DO OVER

A STEAMY SINGLE DAD ROMANTIC COMEDY

SERENA BELL

JMG
JELSBA
MEDIA
GROUP

For BellGirl and BellBoy, for having been so ridiculously adorable at age four, and for Mr. Bell, who possesses, among many, many lovable traits, an infinite willingness to answer the question "Why?"

1

JACK

Chase waves a set of tickets under my nose. "Pac-12 basketball championship. Huskies versus Cougars. Fourth row courtside."

Chase has joined my work buddy Henry and me for lunch today. Henry and I are taking a break from our construction job, and the three of us are sitting on a newly poured retaining wall in the watery Pacific Northwest spring sunshine.

The tickets are close enough that I can smell the sharp tang of the paper and ink, and holy fuck, do I want those tickets. I can feel the energy in the arena, taste the beer and dogs, hear the crowd noise. I don't just want those tickets, I need them.

It's been that kind of week.

Work has sucked balls, with stupid shit going down on the job site, like a built-in bookshelf the client claims is the wrong width and no paper trail to back me up. I got reamed by my boss, and I'm all about washing out the bad taste with beer and basketball.

Henry must read the longing on my face. "Plus. You need to get laid," he adds.

"He's not going to get laid at a basketball game," Chase scoffs.

"You don't know Jack as well as I do," Henry says loyally. "He could get laid in a paper bag.

I roll my eyes. Henry's faith in my powers is outsized—but not totally misplaced. And I have to admit, the thought of taking home a ready-and-willing woman only adds to the appeal.

"I'm in," I say, just as my phone buzzes in my pocket. I pull it out.

And...

It's Maddie.

SOS. Any chance you could take Gabe tonight? Last minute sitter cancellation. Work event. I can drop him with you.

I cast one last longing look in the direction of those basketball tickets. Timing's a bitch—but I made myself—and my kid, indirectly—a promise, and even NCAA championship ball can't sway me.

"Scratch that," I tell the guys. "I'm out."

Henry grabs my phone out of my hand. "This better be a booty call." He reads the text and turns an outraged expression on me. "Tell her no!"

I shake my head. "Sorry, man. Priorities."

Henry and I have been friends since junior high school. He's my wingman—always has my back. He's funny as shit. If I come to work in a bad mood, he's guaranteed to snap me out of it. The only thing is, he can be a bit of a dick about Gabe. I think it's because he's not a dad. He doesn't know what it's like, how everything changes the minute you lay eyes on your mini-me.

Chase shoots me a look of solidarity. He's got a kid, too, and since her mom died several months ago, he's been single-dadding it. He gets how it works, and what matters.

"You got a babysitter?" I ask.

"Yup." He grins like he won the lottery. Which given how hard it is to find sitters, and the fact that he's totally on his own with his kid—no mom, no local family—he definitely has.

Henry scowls at me. "Tell Maddie it's too late! You're already busy!"

I shake my head. "I'm not turning down Gabe time. I'm just starting to claw my way back into his good graces."

Chase, who hasn't known me as long as Henry, furrows his brow. "Wait. Into your kid's good graces?"

I sigh. "I fucked up with him. Big time. When he was a baby, Gabe was a colicky mess. And I couldn't soothe him. I thought it was because he wanted the boob, but then either my mom or my sister would grab him out of my arms and he'd calm right down. Pretty soon they were at my house every time Gabe was. They loved the shit out of him, too, so I just let it happen. Sometimes Maddie would even drop Gabe at my mom's place instead of at my house."

Chase is nodding sympathetically. "Been there," he says. "I let Thea do everything, because she was good at it. And by the time I realized how much I'd withdrawn..."

His voice trails off.

"Let's just say it would have been a hell of a lot easier for both Katie and me to pick up after Thea died if I'd been more involved all along."

I lay a hand on his shoulder. He casts a grateful glance my way.

I nod. "Yeah, well. That's the thing. It kind of slid, you know? Gabe freaked out every time he was at my house, so he ended up mostly at my mom's. When he got a little bigger, he started refusing visits with me, kicking up a big stink. Turned out he was super scared of one of the stuffed toys at my house, but we didn't know that. Maddie canceled on me a bunch, and I didn't push back."

I shrug, like it's not a big deal—but it *is* a big deal. And Chase gets it. His face is still soft with understanding, which is why I'm still talking.

I rake a hand through my hair. "I got a wakeup call a couple weeks ago when Gabe heard my mom and sister calling me 'Jack,' so he called me that, too, instead of 'Daddy.' And no one corrected him. And why should they? I wasn't acting like a dad. I was a fun uncle."

Even as I say it, I feel the old insecurity surface. My own dad was a total fucking asshole. Who's to say I'll ever be good at this Dad thing?

"It's not too late," Chase says.

His confidence helps me shake off the self-doubt. "That's what I realized. So I started stepping it up. Maddie calls? I answer. Any opportunity to be with Gabe? I take it. Get things back to the way they're supposed to be."

It's Chase's turn to rest a hand on my shoulder.

"If this meeting of the Single Dads Survival Club is ready to adjourn," Henry intones darkly.

"Don't be an asshole," Chase tells him. "Jack's trying to do the right thing."

I don't really blame Henry. He just doesn't know what

happens when your genes look back at you through big puppy dog eyes and chubby little kid cheeks.

I love the shit out of Gabe. He's the cutest four-year-old on earth—and I don't say that just because he totally looks like me. He's got those big eyes and a nose that wrinkles up when he's confused, and he is always, always asking questions with his not-quite-right pronunciations of words.

And these questions? They're hilarious.

Henry clears his throat. "So—bottom line, you're out for basketball?"

"I'm out," I confirm.

"No nookie for you," he says grimly.

"No nookie for me," I confirm, only mourning it a tiny bit.

"What could Maddie possibly be doing that's more important than the Pac-12 tourney?"

She didn't tell me, only that it was work-related. And now I'm wondering about Maddie's evening. What's she up to on a Friday night? Is her asshole boyfriend escorting her? Will he be with them tonight when she drops Gabe off?

Will she be dressed up when she drops him? One of her skin-tight, low-cut tops?

Stop it, Jack, I warn myself, because wanting to be a better dad is a noble goal, but wanting anything when it comes to Maddie?

Is an emotional suicide mission.

Just then, my phone buzzes.

Jack? I need an answer.

I hesitate one more second. Not because I'm confused about what matters. As tempting as drowning this shit-heap of a week is, Gabe's more important.

No, I hesitate because I know that my motives aren't

completely pure. Yes, I want to kill off the ghost of my sad-sack old man. I want to do the right thing by Gabe. And I want to be—to the best of my ability—a good father.

But also? I want to prove to Maddie that I've got this.

And that worries me. See above: emotional suicide mission.

I text her back: *Just let me know what time.*

I get a thumbs up, a smile, and a heart.

Fuck me if that last one doesn't make my own stutter.

God damn it, Jack, you will *never* learn.

Chase says, "You're a good man, Jack."

"Thanks." I have my doubts, but I appreciate his faith.

"You're an idiot, Jack," Henry mutters.

"Love you too, man," I tell him.

I'm still thinking about Maddie as I head home in my pickup a couple of hours later. The site where we've been building is three miles from my house, but the town where I live has changed a lot in the last couple of years.

Five years ago, Revere Lake looked pretty much like it did when we were kids: a small main street with a market, a diner, a couple of coffee shops, and stores catering to lake tourism. Now there are new cookie-cutter developments everywhere and box retailers popping up. The city council, in its infinite wisdom, decided it would be a good idea to widen the main drag and put in traffic lights.

End result? It takes twenty minutes for me to make what should be a five-minute commute home.

So I'm late to meet Maddie. Again.

I finally turn off Route 132 and round the last couple of corners. Maddie's little red Toyota Prius is in my driveway, and she and Gabe are sitting on my front steps.

I jump down from the truck and call out, "Hey."

Gabe comes running from her side. I open my arms and he jumps up. I give him a hug. "How are you, buddy?"

"Good! We gon' play football?" He wriggles in my arms and I set him down, catching a whiff of the clean shampoo scent of his hair. How do little kids smell so good?

"Of course!" I tell him. There are about ten more minutes of daylight, but we'll make it work. If there's one thing I'm determined about, it's that Gabe will know how to throw and catch every kind of ball there is before he goes to kindergarten.

I've actually had to talk Maddie into signing him up for sports—soccer, T-ball, pee-wee flag football—which floors me. You can suck at anything else in life, but if you have a passable knowledge of sports, you can survive boyhood. I should know; sports was about the only thing I was ever good at. I'm hoping Gabe will turn out to have Maddie's brains, but if not, at least I'll give him the tools he needs not to get eaten alive.

"The football's in the garage—you want to go get it?" I ask him, and he runs off.

That leaves Maddie and me alone, and I get my first real look at her. She looks *good.* Maddie cleans up great, anyway, but this is another level. She's wearing skinny jeans and a scoop-neck red shirt that bares the tops of her breasts and shiny red boots with spike heels. My brain serves up a quick, dirty flash of what she'd look like wearing those boots and nothing else. Unfortunately, I have never been able to get out of my head how good she looks naked, so it's a vivid picture, right down to how pink her cheeks get when she's turned on.

That ship, however, sailed a long time ago, so I do my best to draw a curtain over the mental pictures.

"So," she says, breaking the silence. "Everything good with you?"

"Yeah. Good as it gets. You?" No way I'm going to tell her about my shitty week or that I turned down an NCAA championship game for this gig. A real man shuts his trap and does the right thing—without needing a medal for it.

"Things could be worse." She shrugs.

We both shift our stances awkwardly. You'd think two people who have a kid in common would eventually find some comfortable way to deal with drop-offs and pickups, but I guess the water under our particular bridge is just that muddy. It's pretty crazy when you think about all the history we have and all the talking we did, once upon a time. But we were just kids then.

"Um, so, overnight bag—" She points to where it's sitting on my stoop. "He's been tough to get to bed lately. I have to read him a lot of stories. He's really liking *Frog and Toad* right now . . ." Her forehead wrinkles.

"We're gonna be fine," I assure her.

She bites her lower lip. That lower lip is a work of fucking art, and when she gets her teeth into it like that, I forget about the muddy waters and just want to soothe the spot she's bitten with my thumb. Or my tongue.

Curtain on that, too.

"Don't let him eat too much sugar."

She says that every time.

"And don't let him stay up too late."

Ditto on that one. I give her a look, and she raises her chin obstinately. "I'm his mom. I gotta say it."

I don't say, *And I'm his dad.* Because although I am—never doubted Maddie's word on that for a second, and if I had, one look at Gabe would have cleared it right up—I need to get back to feeling like I've earned the title.

It scares the shit out of me that if I don't, someday, Maddie might want Gabe to call some other guy, like Harris—her boyfriend—Daddy.

This is not a thought I want to spend any time with, so I change the subject. "Where are you going?" I ask her. The heaped-up curves at the scoop of her shirt are distracting. *Eyes up.*

"My boss is retiring and we're throwing him a party."

"Is Big Dick going with you?"

"Don't call him that."

I've never actually told her this, but I call Harris that because I can't think of any reason she'd be with him other than that he must have a big dick. Otherwise, he has no redeeming features. Well, maybe money. He's a product marketing manager at a biotech company and he's older than we are—thirty-three, I think—and they live together in a condo that's, like, three times as big as my house. But he's one of those guys that just annoys you right away, always knowing everything and having to explain it all, and he interrupts her, which I fucking *hate.*

"*Harris* is working."

"Did he see you in that shirt?"

That slips out before I can think better of it. My better self, in general, fails me around Maddie, which is why I usually keep these meetings as short and sweet as possible.

"What's that got to do with anything?" she demands. Which I know means he did.

This is another reason Harris is a Big Dick. What kind of guy could take even one look at Maddie—especially in that shirt, which is all over her curves like a second skin—and decide he'd rather be *working*? But if I say that to her she'll just get pissed at me. I know from past experience. Harris the Big Dick is a nice guy, Maddie says. If I would just get to know him I'd see that.

Yeah, that's going to happen. When the Cougs win the Pac-12.

Gabe comes back with the football. The small one. He can't even really hold onto the full-sized one yet.

"Right here," I tell him.

He throws it to me. For a guy who's barely four years old, he has a great arm. We really have to work on his spiral, though. It's a wobble at best.

"So—I should go," Maddie says.

"Yeah."

We don't hug, because, muddy waters. Still, I feel like I want to say something, do something, to make it less awkward.

"Tell your mama goodbye," I say to Gabe. "Tell her she looks pretty."

She has just started to crouch over him to hug him good-bye, and she looks up at me, startled.

She has green eyes and high-arched eyebrows that make her look like she's always about to ask a question. Her mouth is a wide bow and her bottom lip—yeah. You already know that drill.

I shrug. "Teaching him how to get the ladies."

She glares at me.

I grin back.

She sighs, and I can tell she's trying not to smile.

There. Tension broken.

"Be a good boy," she tells Gabe, crouching down to hug him, giving me a quick mouthwatering glimpse down her shirt.

"'Bye, Mama," he says. "You pitty!"

I can't read the look on her face when she glances up at me. But that's nothing new. Maddie's been a closed book to me for so long now I almost forget that it wasn't always that way.

She straightens up, gives me a little wave, and takes off across the lawn.

Her dark hair swings, her hips sway, her jeans hug her. She looks just as good going as coming.

2

JACK

It goes smoothly for a while. Gabe and I work on his spiral. It's tough to throw a spiral when your hand is that little. And the small football is weird—there's something off about the weight, and it won't really spiral. He doesn't get frustrated, though. He just keeps throwing one after the other, and sometimes he says, "Pitty good!"—and other times he says, "Better wuck nex' time!" Not sure where he learned that, but it's damn cute.

Then I make him mac and cheese, which is where the trouble starts.

"I want the white kind."

"This is the kind I have," I say, holding up the Kraft box.

"Mommy makes the white kind."

"Daddy makes the orange kind," I say.

"No no no. The *white* kind."

Pretty sure he's about to throw the mother of all temper tantrums.

I take a deep breath. Maddie would know what to do

here. My mother would know what to do. My sister would know what to do.

The man formerly known as my dad, during the brief time he was actually holding that fake title, would have roared his rage and sent me to my room without dinner.

Me? I should know what to do, but I didn't step up when I needed to, and now I'm behind the ball.

Man up, Jack.

I'm gonna have to improvise.

"What about pizza?"

He brightens. "Yeah! Pizza!"

So we order pizza. Crisis averted. Not sure what the child care books would have to say about that, but whatever.

After dinner, I help him get into his pajamas and then we tackle the tooth-brushing. He can sort of brush his teeth by himself but he does a craptastic job, and then he's pissed when someone tries to get the spots he's missed. Way too often, Sienna or my mom has offered to take on this battle— and I haven't refused.

That ends today.

"Gabriel International Airport. This is air traffic control! We have a flight, flight Tooth-Tooth-Nine coming in for a landing..." I circle his face with the toothbrush.

Delighted, he opens his mouth, and I get as many teeth clean as I can before he realizes that I've tricked him and clamps down on the brush with his teeth.

I'm calling it a win.

I get him tucked into the twin bed in his room and sit on the edge. I read him every book Maddie packed for him. Six of them. Then I kiss him good night and shut off the light and close the door most of the way behind me. I leave the light on in the hallway and the bathroom. I know to do that much. Honestly, I remember what it felt like to be a kid, lying in the dark, grateful for that strip of light I could see around the door.

I lower myself to the couch and turn on the TV. The game is on and the Huskies are down 54-42. If I'd been there, they'd be winning. Also, I'd have a beer in my hand and my eye on the prize.

The prize, in the fantasy that flashes through my brain, looks an awful lot like Maddie. For fuck's sake. What is it going to take to erase her? Obviously not pure volume, because I've tried that, and it doesn't change anything. If anything, it only makes it clearer that no one else is Maddie.

"Daddy? I can't sleep."

"Buddy, you were only in bed three seconds," I say, but even as the words are coming out of my mouth, I'm realizing you can't argue like that with a four-year-old. I take a deep breath. "Okay," I say. "Let's go back to bed and try again."

I walk him back down the hall and we start over. We read three of the books again, I tuck him in, and I repeat the same steps with the good-night kiss and the lights out.

This time I've barely lowered myself to the couch when he appears.

"I can't sleep."

How do you get a kid to stay in bed and try sleeping? I've got nothing. I rise to my feet again—Jesus, I'm tired—and lead him back down the hall. "Can you read numbers?" I ask him. I point to the clock.

"Five."

The clock says 8:21, so I don't think that's going to do us any good. I sigh.

"Where's Mommy?"

"She's at a party," I say.

"Where's Grandma?"

"She's in San Francisco."

"Where's Aunt Sienna?"

"She's in New York."

It's a who's who of people who might actually know how the fuck to get a kid to go to sleep, and he's got this look on his face like he's thinking very hard about crying.

"C'mon, bud," I say. There's something tight as hell in my chest; I don't like it.

I reread two books and try again.

The gap between the Beavs and the dogs has widened. Beer will help. I go into the kitchen, crank open a bottle of Heineken, and settle back on the couch. The beer tastes like the nectar of the gods. I feel only slightly guilty for drinking it, until:

"Daddy."

I feel a small surge of irritation, and I instantly think of my father. Getting in my face. Shouting so close I could feel his spit hit my skin, sting my eyes. Slamming doors and hitting walls and calling up a ball of anger and fear and loathing in my gut.

I take a deep breath, and then another. Just because I'm annoyed doesn't mean I'm my dad.

You got this, Jack.

What do I do when I can't sleep?

Don't. Answer. That.

But the thought has done the trick; I'm rolling my eyes at myself and my right-handed bedtime ritual instead of worrying that I'll yell at my kid. Of course, Gabe is nowhere near old enough for that—what did I used to do when I couldn't sleep as a kid?

And then I have a brilliant idea. I lead him down the hall again, tuck him in, and turn on the clock radio—a relic from my own childhood. I spin the dial till I find the game.

"You can listen to basketball," I say.

His eyes get huge.

Twenty minutes later I peek in on him and he's sacked out, snoring his buzzy little-man snores.

I'm helping myself to a (triumphant) second Heineken when I hear a knock at the front door.

It's Maddie.

She's crying.

"Jesus, Maddie, you okay?"

I take a step closer to her. And then one back. Because— she's crying. Which is *exactly* how she and I got ourselves into this situation in the first place.

I'm six two. I weigh two hundred pounds. I work with big tools, including power tools, and most of the time I wear jeans or Carhartts and work boots. For exercise, I lift weights or shoot hoops or toss a football with the guys, maybe play softball if it's summer and the contractor I'm working for has an "office" league going, and for fun I watch sports and NASCAR and drink.

In short, I carry the man card.

Therefore, there is *no excuse for what a sucker I am when it comes to women crying.*

Tears and makeup are running down Maddie's face in

dark streaks, and if Gabe weren't asleep in the bedroom behind me I'd be sure something awful had happened to him. My chest wrings a little at the thought, but I push it away. Can't go there.

"What is it? Is it your mom?"

She shakes her head. Actually, she's shaking all over. "No one. No one's hurt," she manages. "It's not that."

I'm relieved. When I think about Maddie's mom, what I always remember is how she used to make us Nutella sandwiches on white bread when we were little, sit us down in the kitchen and talk to us like we were real people. Like I was worth her time.

Maddie shudders.

"Shh." I stroke her arms, the warmth of her skin rising through the thin layer of her shirt and seeping into my palms. My fingers graze the side of her body, the curve of her breast. *Fuck me.* I take a step back, but it's too late. The feel of her softness is zapping around in my body like the steel ball in a pinball machine. This is why I don't hug Maddie, why I never touch her if I can help it.

"You were right," she wails.

"About what?"

"I shouldn't have moved in with him without a ring."

Harris. That *fucker.* I don't know what he's done yet, but I can feel my fight-or-flight response—meaning the fight part —going into high gear. It would give me so much pleasure to rearrange his face. "What'd he do?"

She hesitates.

"What'd he do?"

She doesn't want to tell me, probably because it's bad and she knows I'm going to lose my shit.

"I came home and he was—" She takes a deep breath. "He was—goingdownonMiainthekitchen."

She strings the words together, so it takes me a minute to pull them apart. But then I get it, and oh, holy fucking Jesus, that's bad.

What's crazy is I didn't see it coming. Harris, yeah. He's a total dickwad, as previously mentioned. This new evidence of assholery barely even counts as a surprise. But Mia, Maddie's best friend? I never saw her as the type to screw Maddie over like that . . .

And man, Jesus, that would hurt. I try to picture Henry doing something like that to me, but I can't. Guy code.

"Those assholes. Jesus, Maddie, I am so sorry."

There are tears streaming down Maddie's face.

Shit. Shit, shit, shit.

I can't just stand here like a gorilla with my hands at my sides and watch her cry.

Plus Maddie's tears make the middle of my chest feel soft and gooey.

Don't do it.

Don't fucking do it, Jack.

It's just like that day five years ago. Just the same.

"C'mere," I say roughly.

Bad idea. Bad, bad, bad idea.

She takes a step forward, into my arms, and I wrap her up. At first it's fine. I pat her back and stroke her hair, and it's okay. I concentrate on the fine, silky feel of her hair and not any of the other places where her body is touching mine.

"He's an asshole, Maddie. He's not worth it. He's not worth being upset over."

She's shuddering and sobbing, and I'm holding her and telling her it's going to be okay.

"They've both been working so much, and I'm such an idiot. I should have been suspicious—"

"Well, yeah, maybe, because Harris is a gigantic dick, but on the other hand, you don't think that your boyfriend and your best friend are going to do the dirty in your kitchen," I say darkly.

That makes her sob even harder. Possibly it wasn't the right thing to say.

"I thought—I thought he was going to *propose* soon. Oh, my *God,* I'm an idiot, Jack, I'm such an idiot."

"You're not an idiot."

God, keep me away from Harris Stoughton so I do not have to go to prison for life for murder.

If she was a little bit of an idiot for thinking that a guy like Harris cared about anything other than his own ego and his (obviously tiny) dick, then it was an easy mistake to make, because any self-respecting guy in his right mind should value her exactly the way she wants and deserves.

As I'm thinking that, my arms tighten around her, my fingers sinking deeper into her hair. I was so right about what a bad idea this is. As soon as her body is flush with mine, as soon as I can feel her heat through her thin shirt and my T-shirt, my heart speeds up and that jolt goes through me, the way it always does when we're touching. Like she's an injection of something rushing through my whole body, super-concentrated where my dick is now hardening between us.

To review: gooey chest, hard dick. Never ends well.

Why do women have to smell so fucking good? And the worst part is, she smells exactly the same as she did the last time I held her in my arms and comforted her like this, the night Gabe was conceived. If you have sex with someone, and it's good, the way it was with Maddie and me, the way she smells gets permanently tattooed into your brain and for the rest of time, that scent is instant-boner territory. You could be walking by some neighbor's garden and *whoosh!* Hard enough to hammer with.

In Maddie's case, I think it's something she puts in her hair, flowery, but not too sweet. But underneath that, something cinnamon that I swear is just her skin. I have never wanted to lick a woman's skin besides Maddie's.

Meanwhile, I've become hyperaware of the part of my body that's sandwiched between us. I'm a big guy—all over—but I think I've just found a few millimeters I haven't been using. Her soft tits are pressed between us, too. All I'd have to do is slide my hands down and around, and I'd have two overflowing handfuls of Maddie. It actually makes my thumbs twitch with the urge to flick over her nipples.

Don't be an asshole, Jack.

I recall having a similar series of thoughts on the night Gabe was conceived.

Now would be a good time to step away.

Because I've been down this road before. In fact, the parallels between the night we made Gabe and tonight are eerie. Including the way my brain is trying desperately to argue that getting a taste of Maddie will be worth whatever comes next. And there's just no way. If the carnival of fuckery that followed the last time we had sex couldn't convince me of that, nothing could. There's no such thing as a free lunch. There's no such thing as getting a taste of Maddie and walking away unscathed.

Her crying has calmed down; she's quiet now in my arms. Just breathing a little fast.

She's just breathing fast because she's upset.

If you take advantage of her right now, you're a bigger dick than Harris.

I'm about to let her go. She's calm now. I'll get her a beer; we'll sit together and watch the rest of the game. She can sleep on the couch and then in the morning she can figure out her plan.

Life will go on, just the way it has. The only way it can.

Then I feel her hip. Just a little nudge.

Against my hard-on.

No way was it deliberate.

But tell that to my dick and the sudden dryness in my mouth and the heat in my chest and the surge of adrenaline through my whole body.

No way was it deliberate.

But there it is again. Harder. Her hip, tipping up against the part of me that wants more than anything to be closer to her. Inside her.

And then she tilts her face up and slides her hand up the back of my neck to pull my head down.

3

———————

MADDIE

Blame sexual drought.

Blame crushed ego and stupid pride.

Blame Jack, for being hot. For answering the door in worn jeans that ride low on his hips and a T-shirt that strains around his biceps and across his shoulders and chest.

Blame Jack for smelling good. Laundry soap and spicy deodorant and heavy cotton and fresh wood shavings and sun-kissed skin.

Blame Jack's erection, which I can feel against my hip and belly as soon as I step close to him. Which returns us, once again, to crushed ego and stupid pride. *Jack wants me, even if Harris doesn't.*

But overall, I think most of the blame lies with the way Jack has always made me feel, as if he's the living embodiment of *It's okay.* No matter how much hurt and heartbreak he's caused me, the connection between us, the sense that with a touch or a few words he can smooth away anything awful in the world, has never gone away. That's part of what makes it so hard to know that Jack will never be my island of safety in the world—that he's never wanted to be—because he's the only man who's ever made me feel like this.

Fifteen minutes ago, I thought I was going to choke on the heartbreak and anger and loneliness I was feeling. I thought it wasn't possible to feel any worse than I felt. I was thinking, *Life changes so fast. It goes to shit in seconds flat.*

I'd left the retirement party two hours earlier than I'd planned, thinking Harris would be home and he and I could kick back on the couch with glasses of wine and reconnect, catch up on what was going on in each other's lives. And yeah, if that led to sex, I wouldn't turn it down. It had been way too long. We'd both been working too hard. When I wasn't working, Gabe was almost always around.

Or that's what I'd told myself was the reason for the sexual drought. Don't parents always have trouble finding time for sex? That's a thing, right?

I drove home from the party, took the elevator to our floor, and unlocked the door of the condo we shared, which somehow I still thought of as "Harris's condo." I was figuring Harris would be sitting on the couch, reading or watching TV, but when I took a few steps forward to where the foyer opened out into the main area, the first thing I saw was my best friend, Mia, in the kitchen. I was thrilled to see her, because she'd been working just as much as Harris, so I didn't think to question why she was in my kitchen. She'd been busy, busy, busy for weeks, and I'd missed her.

Mia and Harris both work at a biotech company, BioMere, which is how I met Harris in the first place—he's Mia's boss. The drug they're marketing is about to launch, so it's been all hands on deck all the time. It's supposed to get better in a few months, but in the meantime, lately, I've been minus a boyfriend and minus a best friend. Because work.

Or that's what I told myself.

Mia was slumped over my kitchen counter with a look on her face that I immediately interpreted as the agony of despair. I called out, "Mia, hon, are you okay?" I thought maybe something had gone horribly wrong with work, and I took off jogging toward her.

As I came around into the kitchen, several things happened at once. Mia straightened and the expression on her face turned to genuine horror, and my field of vision got confused for a moment because it looked like there was something moving under her flowing black skirt, and I was working really hard to make sense out of all these questions that my brain was firing at me:

What is wrong with Mia?

Why is she in my apartment when I am not (a question that has suddenly jumped to the forefront of my brain)?

What is happening under Mia's skirt?

Where is Harris?

And then suddenly my confusing visual experience began to sort itself out as the chaos under Mia's skirt emerged and resolved itself into Harris.

Holy shit.

That wasn't the agony of despair on Mia's face. That was an *O* face caused by *my boyfriend giving her head under her skirt in my kitchen while I was out at my boss's retirement party.*

Harris and I had been together eighteen months, almost half of Gabe's life, living together for the last six months. And if you'd asked me yesterday, I would have told you that Harris and I were one good, long conversation away from engagement and marriage and him becoming Gabe's stepdad.

Apparently I was missing some key details. And my heart just—flew apart. The first thing I thought was, *Oh, my God, I have to tell—*

Mia.

Like a one-two punch.

The two of them closed in on me, surrounding me, talking, both at the same time, making these pointless, meaningless apologies, and the worst part was the way they kept meeting each other's eyes, looking for comfort and confirmation.

Comfort and confirmation that used to be mine.

That's how your life goes to shit in a minute.

But the thing is, it works the other way, too. A minute ago, everything was shit. But now I'm in Jack's arms, and I'm aware of the fact that his body approves heartily of mine. And I'm feeling that—despite everything cataclysmic that's just happened—*it's okay. Because that's how Jack makes me feel. That's how Jack has always made me feel.*

All I want is more of him. Because Jack also makes me greedy. I want his mouth on mine and that excellent, admirable erection inside me (where I know from personal experience that it will rock my world), and despite our track record and the fact that having Jack makes me crave more Jack and that Jack is not remotely, even slightly, available for the having, I can't resist the craving.

There's some part of my brain shouting desperately out of the snake pit, *Don't do it! You're on the rebound!*

But that sane voice gets drowned out. Somehow, my hand

is on the back of his head, in his hair (soft, wavy), and I'm pulling him down to me.

His lips barely touch mine at first, and I can feel him tug back, resisting, and for a second I think he's going to reject me. And I know this is stupid and immature, but I can't take it right now. I selfishly need him to cancel out the awful feeling of having the two people who are supposed to love you most in the world betray you and make you feel like you don't matter *at all.* Right now, I'm not thinking about any of the reasons this is a bad idea. I'm just thinking about how his body is telling me I'm okay—I'm safe. I'm sexy. I matter, in some way, even if it's a shallow way.

So I beg. "Please, Jack."

It's like all his resistance just collapses. His mouth settles onto mine and his arms come tighter around me, and we're kissing.

His lips are so knowing. And he takes control, right away, setting the pace—slow, with a sweet edge of desperation. His tongue inquires at the seam of my lips and I open to him because there's really no question. I'm open to him and I always have been. I can't close him off, not completely—not the way I've wished so many times I could.

I go from wanting to be wanted to just pure *want,* and he's the same. We're all over each other. I weave my fingers in his hair and he tugs a handful of mine. I grab his butt to pull him tighter against me and he picks me up so I can wrap my legs around his waist, and then he's carrying me over to the couch and setting me down, laying me down, covering me, still kissing me, kissing my face, my neck, the vee of my shirt, the tops of my breasts. He tugs at my shirt and I pull it up over my head and he groans.

"Oh, my *God,* Maddie."

You see? a different voice in my head says. *He thinks you're beautiful.*

He goes after me with hands and mouth, tugging down the lace of my bra, dipping his head to nip and flick my nipples, telling me I have the most perfect breasts ever (which cannot be true—I have nursed a baby—but whatever). Lower down, his body is moving very slowly and gently and deliberately against mine, not just rock and thrust, which would be bad enough, but with this sweet crazy friction across the seam of my jeans that will, if he keeps it up, make me come screaming his name.

"Jack," I whimper.

"Mmm?"

"Don't stop."

"Not a chance."

He's not kidding, either. He keeps it up, just like that, that perfect rhythm, that perfect friction, until I bow my whole body from the intensity of it and bite—hard—into his shoulder. And even then, he doesn't flinch away, doesn't stop, just says, "Yeah, that's it, that's right, baby, you come for me."

Then I can do nothing but lie like a limp rag on his couch and watch as he strips his T-shirt off and begins to unbutton and unzip his jeans. I know that underneath those jeans is Just Jack, although there is nothing Just about Jack at all. I'd blocked that bit, maybe out of self-preservation, because when you're sleeping with someone who's giving you 75 percent of the max you've had, it doesn't pay to dwell on what you're missing.

But now my full attention is on the lovely, lovely surplus

that is about to be unveiled for me. Memory has flooded back: behind that fly, he's long and straight and thick and—

Then he freezes, and something goes cold in my chest.

He stays like that for a moment, still as a statue. And then he shakes his head.

"Jack," I beg.

His hand goes to his fly again, but I can tell something's changed.

"I was going to do it again," he says. "I was going to fuck you without a condom, *again*."

He shakes his head like he's disgusted with himself. And then he turns the look of disgust on me. "You don't want this," he says.

"I—"

But I'm not sure exactly what I am going to say. Am I going to tell him that what just happened felt more right than being with Harris ever felt?

Or that Jack, after all these years, can still make everything okay, just by being Jack?

Or am I about to tell him he's right, that I kissed him, made him kiss me, because I was on the rebound and needed someone to make me feel like I mattered?

Which is also, clearly, true.

Down the hall, there's a small cry, barely more than a whimper.

Jesus. Gabe!

In a flash, Jack's got his jeans zipped and buttoned and is heading down the hall.

I feel a hot burst of shame and remorse for having let this happen. With Gabe asleep down the hall, no less. It doesn't matter that Gabe cries out like that all the time and almost never actually wakes up. I didn't even check on him to make sure he was sleeping. That's how in my own head—or maybe it's more accurate to say, how possessed by my own body—I was.

I pull myself to sitting, and everything feels wrong and sordid. My rumpled clothes, *my boots still on,* my hair tangled and sweaty, the damp crotch of my panties and jeans, the slight sensation of burn from the friction of his rubbing.

I was going to do it again, he'd said.

I was going to fuck you without a condom again.

It's that little word, *again,* that restores me to my senses. Because it brings it all home. The fact that we've been here once before, and we both know, all too well, that it doesn't get us anywhere. Jack is Jack, as he so abundantly proved to me five years ago. He is a sucker for tears, a comforter par excellence, a lover of whatever woman is naked and vulnerable in his den, but he's *not* husband material.

He doesn't have to be, a wicked little voice whispers. *You could just let him make you feel good.*

The real problem, however, is that there is no "just" with Jack. That's the real lesson I learned the last time I tried this. That when I have some Jack, I want *all the Jack.* I want him to touch me, yes, I want him to make me come like he just did—harder than anyone ever has, without even half-trying. But even more than that, I want him to be part of my life. I want him to be part of our lives.

But that is not a thing that exists.

At least, not for me and Gabe.

4

———

JACK

Gabe is still snoring away. He must have been dreaming.

I come back down the hall, and she's sitting on the couch, and her body language screams it: we're not going to have sex. Clothes neat, back straight, legs crossed, hands folded. *Closed for business.*

Yeah. Probably for the best.

Said no man, ever. I am still craving access to her body like a starving man craves food, but even a starving man can recognize an empty pantry.

"So," I say.

Her eyes fill with tears again. "I—I'm sorry."

"What are you apologizing for?"

"For letting things go so far and then not—"

She gestures in the general direction of my waning semi.

"Getting me off?" I shrug. "I'm a big boy. I can take it."

Notice, I don't apologize. Not that I don't feel a little bit guilty for letting her jump me when she wasn't in her right mind. But only a little bit. That was her hand on the back of my head and her voice murmuring, *Jack, please,* and her whimpering *Jack, don't stop.*

Yeah. I was paying attention. All of me was.

"I was upset—"

"No, *really?*" I say. It comes out testier than I mean it to. I guess I'm just—confused.

"I should go," she says quietly.

I'm not planning to argue with her. Mainly because I'm too busy having an argument in my own head. One part of me—the part that actually knows what's good for itself—is relieved that she's just going to walk away. Because as much as my body has designs on hers, there is no way that won't lead to complications. And I'm not a complications guy. I'm the simplest guy you know. I go to work, I go out with the guys, I pay child support and take care of my kid, I get laid when the urge strikes. It's worked out well for me since Gabe was born, and I was planning on sticking to that strategy for the next seventy years or so.

The other part of me, the crazy, stupid, self-destructive part, is thinking, *Just a little more. Just one night. Or two. Or a week, or a month, or as long as it takes to get this out of our systems. What can it hurt?*

She stands up, the movement sharp and decisive.

"You can't go back there."

This is not a thing I plan to say. It just pops out of my mouth. Because I'm picturing her going back to that condo she shares with Harris. The condo where she found him with his tongue on her best friend's—

Yeah, not so much.

I can see the moment when she has the same realization.

"I can't go back there," she repeats. And her whole upper

body kind of collapses. Her face, too. I recognize that look. It's not unlike the look that Gabe had on his face an hour earlier when he realized that all the women in his life had abandoned him with me.

Don't cry. Please don't cry.

"And I definitely can't stay with Mia."

The way she's cataloguing it, where she can't go, it makes my chest hurt.

"I could—go to San Diego."

Her mom and dad are in San Diego. They retired there right after Maddie moved into Harris's place with Gabe. Maddie complains all the time about how far away her parents are and how infrequently Gabe gets to see them. If she went to San Diego with Gabe, it would break my mom's and my sister's hearts.

"Stay here," I burst out.

I'm not thinking. Because if I'd been thinking, I'd know that was the worst idea ever. The kind of idea dreamed up by a still semi-hard dick frustrated in its evening activities, not by an actual brain. And yet, I'm still talking. Or one of my heads is still talking, anyway.

"I have lots of space. Gabe has a room here."

And we could finish what we just started. We could let it play out, see where it goes. Get it done, get it out of our systems, put it behind us.

You idiot! my brain is shouting back at me. *If you want to get laid, there are twenty women I can think off the top of my head, no strings attached, no complications (and that's not counting the ones you would have met tonight if you'd gone to the game with Chase and Henry). This one? She's off limits. She's always been off limits.*

Maddie's shaking her head. "That's a really bad idea."

"Why?"

Have I mentioned I'm contrary? If someone fights with me, I tend to dig in. It's one of the things that used to send my dad into a rage. Two seconds ago, I was pretty sure it was a really bad idea, too, but now that Maddie's arguing with me—

"It would be confusing for Gabe. Having his parents together."

"Not more confusing than you moving out of Harris's condo. It would be the least disruptive thing for him. If you're going to pull him out of Harris's place, that's going to mess with his head, but at least this is familiar."

I am officially a dick, because I am using emotional manipulation and the happiness of our child to convince a woman to stay under my roof so that I can have another shot at getting her into bed. But I don't feel that guilty. Maybe because I think what I said is actually true. Gabe is going to be super-confused no matter what. He likes Harris (the only example of really bad taste I've seen from him—must be Maddie's genes). So maybe hanging out here for a little bit would make a good consolation prize.

Maddie looks confused now. I can see her working through the details in her head. So I give her a little help.

"Commute stays the same." The pharmacy where she works is in Seattle, so actually halfway between Harris's condo and my house. "It'll give you time to find a place that's the right size and not too expensive, which will save us both money." I figure if I display some obvious self-interest, that will deflect her away from my real self-interest. "Plus, built-in child care."

She eyes me suspiciously.

"What? I'd be here anyway. And my mom and my sister are super close. You know they'd be psyched to help."

"But Gabe's preschool is near Harris's place—"

"So he'll switch. You can pull him out, and either send him near me or wait till you figure out where you're going to live and then enroll him."

She bites her lip, thinking about it. "I think I have to pull him anyway. It doesn't make sense for me to live in Mukilteo if Harris and I aren't together."

The thing is, I have now actually convinced myself it's a great idea. For one thing, where the hell else is she going to go? She doesn't have other friends she's as close to as Mia, and even if she did, they probably wouldn't have the space to take in both her and Gabe. But apart from that, this is actually a good solution for me, because it lets me really get back in the dad game. And it's a great solution for the two of them, for all the reasons I gave her. And there might be a few additional benefits—

Her eyes narrow. It's possible she saw my glance slide over her body when I was thinking about benefits. If I did not mention this earlier, being pregnant and nursing Gabe made Maddie's body sexier. Rounder, more generous, softer—

Eyes up, Jack.

Mine meet hers, unfortunately. *Caught.*

"That—what just happened—" She waves a hand to indicate the couch. "That can't happen again."

I thoroughly disagree with her, but I'm not going to argue. I nod, earnestly. "Okay. That can be a ground rule." We can revisit the ground rules as necessary, later.

She is still eyeing me suspiciously.

"*You're* the one who jumped *me*," I point out.

She looks sheepish, and relaxes a little.

"I'll go make up the guest bed."

"Jack—"

She's going to say no. She's going to say what a bad idea it is—for her, for me, for Gabe, for all of us.

Her eyes are soft, still red from crying earlier, and very green in the lamplight.

"Thank you."

She follows me down the hall and we make up the guest bed together, not talking much, me swearing occasionally under my breath *as one does* over the fact that it's the twenty-first century and no one's managed to come up with anything better than a fitted sheet.

"Can I borrow something to sleep in?" she asks. "I guess I'll have to go back there tomorrow to get some of my stuff at least." Her face crumples at that.

"I can go with you. Run interference."

"You'd do that?"

She doesn't have anyone else to do it. I don't point that out to her, though. I just say, "Yeah."

I give her one of my T-shirts and a pair of sweat shorts with a tie waist. She says she'll use Gabe's toothbrush tonight.

I say, "Um, good night."

She says, "Yeah. Good night."

I brush my teeth and slide between my own sheets.

She's wearing my clothes. They're touching her bare skin.

I lie there, my balls still achy, thinking, *So much for not-a-complications-guy.*

5

─────────

MADDIE

I can't sleep.

It's just too much. The images burned into my mind, of the expression of abandon on Mia's face and the guilt on Harris's, and the way they looked to each other for support. How I figured it out, in jerky frames like a bad filmstrip: *Mia's face. Mia's skirt. Harris. Under the skirt. His head under the skirt, with his face—cheating. My boyfriend's cheating. On. Me. With. My. Best. Friend.*

The woman formerly known as my best friend, that is.

In the dark room, in the quiet house, my thoughts are thick and heavy and my mind won't let any of them go so I can drift off.

When I left the condo, I knew I had to get away. And I knew I needed to go somewhere—somewhere safe—but all I could think of was that Mia and Harris had taken that away from me. They'd taken *home* away from me. They'd taken *trust* away from me.

Except—Jack had done that, years before. So Mia and

Harris were only reminding me that trusting someone to take care of your feelings was a really, really bad idea.

Yet, insanely, when I was sitting in my Prius, gripping the wheel like it would keep me from breaking into pieces, tears running down my face, the only place I could think to go—the only place that still felt safe—was Jack's.

I told myself that part of it was that I wanted to be near the one guy who I knew loved me without reservation: Gabe.

I think that even in my totally wrecked state, I knew that wasn't the whole truth.

And now I know for sure it's not, because even as I'm lying here, my thoughts don't stay fixed on Mia and Harris, what I saw or what I've lost.

They keep wandering to Jack.

It doesn't help that I'm wearing his clothes. It doesn't help that his clothes, and the sheets, and the whole goddamned room, smell like him. Or that my body is still quietly luxuriating in the aftermath of the really, really intense orgasm he gave me. Or that even though I know it's the worst idea on earth, I'm contemplating whether there might be another one in my future.

I should never have agreed to stay here.

Of course, Jack's logic all made sense. Everything he said was true and valid. And I'd already reached the conclusion that I had nowhere else to go. I reached it when I was sitting in my car, trying to figure out where to run. Besides Gabe and Mia and Harris, I had my parents, but I knew San Diego wasn't an option with Gabe asleep at Jack's. I had friends from work and other periods of my life, but I didn't have the kind of relationship with any of them where I could call them late at night and ask to crash for a night—or ten—with my four-year-old son.

(I did make a mental note, sitting in the car, to cultivate more of those kinds of relationships, as a hedge against all the stupid shit that can go wrong. Never again with the one-boyfriend, one-best-friend strategy.)

And then there was Jack.

The first time the idea popped into my head, I dismissed it. I couldn't run to Jack, for a lot of reasons. Our relationship—if you could even call it that—ended when he betrayed me. He made it abundantly clear then, as he had for years before and has for years since, that he didn't want to be tied down or asked to give up his freedom. And I'm still angry, and hurt, by all of that.

But beneath all that—like the good bones of a classic old home that's been through bad renovations—is a very old friendship.

This is one of my earliest memories of Jack:

I was ten. He was eleven. We were lying on the floor of his room on our stomachs, facing each other across a Stratego board. Jack was winning. Jack always won. I kept threatening not to play him anymore, telling him it wasn't fun when he always won, but the truth was, I loved that game and I especially loved playing it with Jack. He made up stories about the pieces, as if they were real soldiers in a real war, and part of why I always lost was that I was listening so hard to his story and feeling so sympathetic for the reluctant spy who had just gotten captured and tortured that I'd forget I was supposed to strategize.

Except that day I wasn't thinking about Jack's story or

strategy because it was thundering outside, and thunderstorms freaked me out.

I'd been scared of lightning for as long as I could remember. My parents had told me a hundred times that the house was safe during a storm, but when a crash of lightning came out of nowhere, it still startled me so bad it left my heart pounding and sent cold water through my veins. And when the lightning and the thunder were right on top of each other, it never mattered to me that I was in the house. I was sure the house was going to be struck and that all the violent bright energy would surge straight through me and burn me to ash.

Jack's mom was out getting groceries. She'd just started leaving us alone when she went out. Jack's older sister was upstairs in her room, so if there had been an emergency, she would have known what to do. *I* would have known what to do. I'd have called 911. Or my mom, who was just one block away—if it wasn't a big emergency.

Is it a big emergency or a little emergency if the house gets struck by lightning?

That's what I was thinking about when the house seemed to crack wide open, the white light and vicious sound shaking me so hard I was sure I'd been hit.

The power went out.

It wasn't pitch dark but, oh my God, my brain felt like it had been shaken and my hands were clenched into fists and someone whimpered and it was me. And I couldn't catch my breath. It kept getting faster and shallower and my chest kept getting tighter and tighter.

Just when I thought I was dying, I felt something. A hand around mine. A hand clutching mine tight, like a raft in the middle of an ocean of fear, and I clutched back. Jack's hand.

And I gradually became aware of the world again. Jack's hand was bigger than my hand, which was a thing I had never noticed before. Jack's hand was warmer than my hand. A lot warmer. Comfort streamed out of Jack's hand and flowed into my cold-water veins. It flushed the ice out and filled me up with Jack's warmth.

"It's okay," he said. And he sounded so sure, I believed him. I forgot all about the thunder and lightning, which were receding now, and I forgot about the fact that the power was out and we were home alone, and I just sat there in the dark with Jack, feeling safe and happy.

So here's the thing. Jack may not be the kind of guy who is meant to be a father or a husband. He may not be capable of monogamy or commitment. But he always was my friend.

That was the realization that brought me here tonight.

And it turns out Jack still is my friend, as evidenced by the fact that I have a warm, safe place to sleep tonight.

At the moment, he is my only real friend.

Quite possibly my last coherent thought before I finally succumb to total exhaustion is: I can't risk damaging my friendship with Jack over sex.

6

———

MADDIE

"**M**ommy?"

I pull back the covers to make way for Gabe, who climbs in next to me and snuggles his face smack up against mine. There is nothing softer or sweeter in the world than a pudgy little kid.

I get about three seconds of pure enjoyment, fat silky cheek against my skin, before everything rushes back from the night before and I groan. It feels a lot like getting kicked in the gut. Again. Tears well up, but I fight them down, because of Gabe.

"What's wrong, Mommy?"

"Nothing, buddy."

There will be time later today for Gabe to learn that his world has been turned upside down. New home, new preschool, goodbye Harris, goodbye Auntie Mia.

On the other hand, more Daddy time and an abundance of Grammy and Auntie Sienna. He might regard it as a decent trade. Gabe can be weirdly philosophical for a four-year-old.

I sigh and crack one swollen eye open. It's 5:45 a.m. I probably got—dunno, two, three solid hours of sleep? It feels like there's a thick, tight band around my chest.

"How'd you know I was in here?"

"Daddy said."

I can picture the scenario without much trouble. Gabe went into Jack's room and woke him up, either by saying his name repeatedly (his usual strategy) or by staring into his face until he woke up (I've been the object of that particular technique many times, and it's always hard not to scream). And Jack, not wanting to be awake at the butt crack of dawn, foisted Gabe off on me and went blissfully back to sleep.

Can't say I'm surprised. Jack may think it's a well-kept secret, but I know for a fact he's almost never alone with Gabe. I know because I read his mother's Facebook page, which Jack, not being on Facebook, probably doesn't give a second thought to. Jack's mother's Facebook page bubbles over with joy at getting to spend time with Gabe, and it's full of adorable pictures of Gabe (which I appreciate) and stories of funny stuff that Gabe has done while she and Sienna, Jack's sister, are watching him. Jack occasionally gets a mention, but it doesn't take a super genius to figure out who's doing the heavy lifting.

I'd be pissed, or sad, or whatever, but Jack never claimed things would be different. That was the one thing he was totally and completely up front about—the fact that father-hood wasn't in his immediate *or* long-term plans. I was surprised at first that he even asked for the every-other-weekend plan—when Gabe was around six months old—until I started seeing the Facebook pages and realized who was really asking for those visits. (And then I was a little mad at myself for ever thinking it might be otherwise. Because just a tiny bit, I'd gotten my hopes up that his asking for those weekends was the beginning of something. Him falling in love with Gabe, with fatherhood, with the idea of family . . .)

I'm glad I got disillusioned quickly. That's the way to go with Jack: quick disillusionment. I should celebrate the fact that each time I make the mistake of hoping things will be different, it takes less time till I remember how stupid that is.

And speaking of illusions and disillusionment: you'd think as a mom I would have realized, oh, say, three years ago, that when your kid climbs into bed with you, it isn't an opportunity to snuggle and drift back into the soft cloud of dreamy morning sleep. It's more like you're the playground and he's getting his morning exercise. Within moments, Gabe is draped over my head, kicking his feet against my stomach.

"Okay, kiddo," I say, dumping him off me and kissing him all over his face. "Let's go get some breakfast."

To my surprise, when we get into the kitchen, Jack is brewing coffee. Blearily, yes—he doesn't look happy about it —but he's awake. He's also wearing nothing but a pair of flannel pajama pants low on his hips. I try very, very hard not to sneak a peek at his bare torso, but fail. You would have failed, too, believe me. Jack is a work of art—broad, muscular chest—taut, tanned—flecked with golden hair, his abs a parade of subtle but distinct ridges and valleys, bisected beneath his navel by that same crisp hair, trending darker. And, because the pants ride low, I get treated to a glimpse of that vee of muscle at his hip, arrowing artfully toward—

When I lift my gaze to his face, he raises both eyebrows and smirks.

Damn it, that was longer than a peek. And Jack is well aware of it.

The whole thing—beautiful view, sexy smirk, Jack's deliberate show and his conscious enjoyment of the results—starts a chain reaction low in my belly.

But nope, nope, nope, not gonna go there. Obviously, it's a bad idea to sleep with someone who's letting you crash at his house, who's the father of your child but not your husband, and who you know will never want more from you than what he's already getting. But on top of that, there's the conclusion I reached last night: I don't have enough friends left that I can afford to screw things up with one of them.

I shake my head to ward off his smirk. "Moment of weakness," I say. "I was serious about what I said last night. No monkey business."

"Monkey business," Gabe says. "No monkey business!"

"You got that right," I tell him.

I deliberately don't look at Jack, certain he's still smirking. Instead I cross to where he keeps the mugs and pull two down.

"Hey, bud," Jack says to Gabe. "How about some pancakes?"

"Yeah!" Gabe crows.

Whereupon I get treated to the best show of the morning, for real: Jack trying to cook pancakes.

I settle myself on a stool with my coffee and watch.

Jack's house is nice. Cozy. Nothing fancy. The kitchen has butcher-block countertops, including an island, plain white cabinets with small metal pulls, a farmhouse-style sink, and a terra-cotta tile floor. Jack redid it himself when he bought the house a couple of years ago. I like it way better than Harris's glass-metal-granite aesthetic.

Harris. I get a shocked, sinking feeling in my gut—that

kick again. For bits at a time, I can forget, and then, wham. For all the ways Harris didn't—can't—live up to Jack, I was with him a year and a half, and he was good to me and Gabe (until he wasn't). I loved him; at least I think I did. He was a harbor in the storm, a grown-up I could talk to, and a source of satisfying if not exceptional sex; and even bigger than all that, I convinced myself that he was going to be there for me and Gabe for all foreseeable future time. I think losing that feels the worst of all, because it was something I never let myself count on before him. The idea that Gabe and I would find a man who wanted to be our family.

Although when I spell it out for myself like that, it doesn't sound so hot. *I think I loved this guy. I could talk to him, the sex was not bad, and he was going to take care of me and my kid.*

I once wanted more than that.

I once believed I could have it.

God, I was naive.

I snap out of my musings to discover that we are surrounded by a cloud of flour.

"You should let Gabe do that," I tell Jack, the author of the flour cloud. "He's good at it."

Jack glares at me.

"Want me to do it, Daddy?"

"I've got it under control," Jack says crisply.

"But you didn't *wevel* it."

"You're teaching a four-year-old to cook?" Jack narrows his eyes.

"Yes. Clearly someone in your house needs to know how to make pancakes."

He gives me a look. I wish I could accurately convey this look. It's level and stern and challenging. He needs to not do that. Which probably means I need to not rib him. There's something in the banter that gets us both going. Always has.

"You show him, Gabe. Show him how it's done."

Gabe takes a knife and draws it surprisingly successfully across the top of Jack's cup of flour. Of course, it's blade side down and he does it over the counter instead of over the flour container, but what do you want? He's four.

I lay off the mockery for a few minutes, enjoying the sight of Gabe and Jack side by side, measuring the other ingredients, until they get to the eggs. Jack tries to break the first one and shatters pieces of shell into the bowl. I watch him try to fish them out, thick fingers sliding through the slippery white, and then I can't watch that anymore, so I tug the bowl toward me and ease the pieces of shell out one by one.

I break the rest of the eggs without getting any shell in the bowl.

Jack plugs in the griddle, then takes the bowl of eggs in one hand and the whisk in the other, and beats the eggs with surprising competence.

And a certain Jack flair.

His forearms are strong, sinewy, ropey. The light hair is crisp at the thick bulge of muscle just below his elbow, fanning out to nearly straight at his wrists.

It occurs to me that Harris made me pancakes all the time but I don't remember ever, once, staring at his forearms like I'd fallen into a trance.

"See something you like?" Jack inquires.

"Just hungry," I lie reflexively.

Shit. I raise my gaze to find him smiling with amusement at me.

"For breakfast," I clarify.

He raises an eyebrow and flicks a speck of water onto the griddle.

It sizzles.

I busy myself finding plates and silverware.

I CROUCH down on the floor of Gabe's room, surrounded by Legos. He just recently graduated from the chunky Duplos to the smaller pieces, and he still struggles to fit the pieces together.

"Buddy, we're going to move to a new apartment soon. Just you and me."

He looks up from where he's sorting the pieces by color and size. "Is Harris coming too?"

I feel awful. Gabe is too little to understand that we have to leave, that I can't stay in a relationship with a man who would do what Harris has just done, that it will be best for both of us in the long run. So I can't give him any kind of explanation for why we have to move out of probably the only home he remembers.

Having to break this piece of news to Gabe is exactly why Jack said I shouldn't move in with Harris without a ring. And not an engagement ring, either. A wedding band. At the time, I'd accused Jack of being old-fashioned, and I'd secretly thought—hoped?—that he was jealous, if not that Harris got to have me, that Harris got to have more time with Gabe.

But Jack was just being practical and looking out for Gabe. I'd been naive, thinking that all the pretty words that Harris said to me ("I want you to move in with me so I can wake up to you every day for the rest of my life," "This is the first step on the path to forever," and so on) meant something. In retrospect, if Harris was so sure of us, it would have been easy for him to make things more permanent.

Idiot.

I know beating up on myself isn't going to change anything, or make the situation any better, but it's really hard not to do it. And I'm super-cynical right now, but all I can think is that what he really wanted was for me to be more conveniently located so he could get laid without having to deal with transportation and child care. Until even that wasn't convenient enough for him . . .

"Harris isn't coming with us," I tell Gabe. I brace myself for his reaction—tears, a temper tantrum.

"Okay," he says, and carefully begins assembling the red squares into a tower.

I blink.

"You can visit him whenever you want."

He looks up from his work and tilts his head to one side. "I don't have to visit him. He's not my daddy."

He resumes his work, but with the blue pieces.

I'm startled. I mean, I've made a point of making sure that Gabe knows that Jack is his dad, of course, but I've also never made a big thing about how Harris isn't. I guess because I was thinking maybe someday (in the very near future, *sigh*) Gabe would think of Harris as more of a father figure than Jack, even.

"Lookit my helicopper," Gabe says, holding it out to me. It does vaguely resemble a helicopter, if only because the topmost piece in his tower has a rotor on it. Then he snatches it out of my hands again and pilots it around the perimeter of the room, making *rrrrrrrrr* noises.

"It's a really great helicopter, bud," I tell him, as he brings it to a landing on the night table. For refueling at the clock radio, apparently. My heart gives a squeeze of love for him, my little guy.

I'm still stuck on his unconcern over Harris not coming with us, but the more I think about it, the more I realize how little of a role Harris really had in Gabe's life. When I was at work, even when Harris wasn't, Gabe stayed with our babysitter, or went to preschool. When both of us were home, Gabe was still my responsibility. I dressed him, fed him, played with him, put him to bed. And the past few months—actually, almost since we moved in—Harris was at work so often he was almost never home when Gabe was awake.

The more I think about it, the more I realize I can't remember the last time Harris spent any time with Gabe.

No wonder Gabe doesn't feel like he's going to miss him.

Thank God, I think. *Thank God this happened now and not four years from now, when Harris and I were married and Gabe was heavily invested in him.*

I may feel like absolute crap, but I haven't ruined my kid's life.

7

———

JACK

At the last minute, Maddie tells me I can't come with her to Harris's. She wants me to stay with Gabe.

"I think it's going to be upsetting to him, seeing me pack all our stuff up," she whispers. We're in the living room. Gabe's in his room with his huge tub of Legos, castoffs from Sienna's and my childhood, open on the floor. He's humming happily to himself while building.

"He can handle it," I remind her. Maddie and I have different ideas about some aspects of parenting. I think she babies Gabe when it comes to emotional stuff. I want my kid to grow up resilient, and it starts right now, with her not treating him like he's fragile.

She hesitates, and I realize: Yeah, she's worried about Gabe's feelings, but there's more to it than that.

She bites her lower lip, one pearly white tooth digging into the soft flesh. "It might be awkward. If Harris has anything he wants to say."

Holy shit, she actually wants to have a conversation with

Harris. She's going to listen to his bullshit explanations and apologies.

The thought bugs the shit out of me. I didn't think he deserved her in the first place. For fucking sure he doesn't deserve two spare minutes of her time after what happened. She should get in there, take whatever stuff of hers and Gabe's she wants, and get the hell out, with as little fanfare as possible. I originally told her she should go when she thought Harris wouldn't be there, but the idea of accidentally walking in on another cozy scene between Mia and Harris was too horrifying to her; she had to text him to let him know she was coming so there was no chance of that happening. Okay, I get that, but I am not down with her actually conversing with the guy, for lots of reasons.

"You're going to let him try to talk his way back into your pants," I blurt. Sometimes stuff just falls out of my mouth. It's not my best trait, but there you have it.

"I'm not," she insists, but she doesn't quite make eye contact. "I just think—it's going to be too weird if you're there."

"Who cares if it's weird? The guy had his face in your best friend's p—" I successfully manage not to finish that sentence. "He doesn't deserve for it not to be weird."

She shakes her head. "It's not that."

"What is it, then?"

She won't look at me.

"I should come with you," I say. "Gabe and I should come with you so you don't have to deal with him alone. That's what you said you wanted last night."

Of course, there were other things Maddie wanted last night, too, but those also evaporated in the light of day.

Shut up.

Just saying.

She gets this look. Squinty, uncomfortable.

"Idon'twantyougettingintoitwithhim."

Takes me a minute.

"I'm not going to 'get into it with him.'" I cross my arms.

Although I'm not completely sure this is true. I'm still having vivid fantasies of introducing his face to my fist. And that's without seeing him however he's going to be—smug or unapologetic or sniveling or—

She's staring at my hands, which seem to have clenched themselves so tight that my knuckles are white. "I rest my case."

Okay, yeah, I hate his fucking guts.

I very slowly release my hands from their fists.

"What if I promise?"

She gives me the side eye.

So I resort to shame. What can I say, I'm a bad man. "Don't flatter yourself that I would mess up my hands over your ex-boyfriend."

She winces.

Too much. *Shit.* But I can't take it back now, especially because just behind that wince I can see her relenting. I've convinced her I'm not going to beat the crap out of Harris. So I shrug and say, "I'll hang back with Gabe. I won't even open my mouth. We'll be good. We'll just be there for moral support."

"Why do you care so much about being there?" she asks, which in light of the stupid thing I just said to her is a perfectly reasonable question.

Since I'm too surprised by the question, I don't have

enough time to come up with some tossed-off nonchalant answer. The best I can manage is the truth. "I don't like the way he treats you. Never have. And I don't want you to go back to him. I don't want you to be tempted to."

It's just a statement. It's the kind of thing that one friend might say to another. In fact, Mia might have said the exact same thing to Maddie. If, say, Harris had been caught with his face between someone else's legs and Mia had been the one Maddie had run to.

(I'm glad that it didn't happen that way, that Maddie ran to me. Which is sick and wrong and makes me a dick, but there you have it.)

Maddie is staring at me like she's trying to figure me out. With a weird uncertain look on her face. And it's making me fidgety.

"I'm your friend, right?" I say. "That's what friends do. They don't let friends make the same stupid mistake twice."

"Right," she says, smirking.

Damn it, walked right into that one.

In the end, Maddie and I compromise. I go with her to Harris's, but she leaves Gabe at my house with his babysitter, who drives from Seattle to watch him. She has a whispered conversation with the sitter, I guess to tell her the gist of what Big Dick did and why she needs someone to watch her kid on a Saturday so she can move out.

I have a very specific image in my head of babysitters, left over from my own preadolescence, so I am disappointed to find that this one is fiftyish and graying, with a potbelly. She's great with Gabe, though—you can tell right away. She's down on the floor making helicopter noises before we're out the door.

Maddie and I stop at U-Haul and buy a bunch of small boxes.

On the drive, she makes a list of all the stuff she wants to make sure she gets from his house. "So I can get in and out fast."

"Good plan."

She gives me a look.

"What!?"

"It sounded dirty."

"Then you have a dirty mind."

She squints at me, then gives up. "It's mostly clothes, shoes, jewelry, personal stuff. My music's on my phone. My books are on my Kindle. I got rid of the few pieces of furniture I had when I moved in with him. They didn't fit with his stuff." She sighs. "Maybe I should have taken that as a sign."

We drive to Mukilteo, a suburb north of the city, which, like Revere Lake, has been getting more developed since Google and Amazon and the rest of Silicon Valley invaded Seattle. Harris lives in a brand-new condo building with views of Puget Sound. Aside from the view, which is awesome, it's the most sterile, soulless building you can imagine. It reminds me of this bumper sticker you see a lot in the Ballard neighborhood of Seattle, where development has surged since the tech boom started and tons of pre-WWII houses have been demolished to make way for condo buildings: *Ballard Welcomes Our New Condo Overlords.*

We ride the elevator up. Maddie hesitates outside the

door. "It's so weird," she says. "I'm about to knock on my own front door."

"Use the key," I say.

She shakes her head, raises her hand, and knocks.

Harris opens the door. He's taller than Maddie but shorter than me, lanky, with black hair that needs a cut. It makes sense in a weird way that Maddie would end up with a guy like him. He looks like all the other nerdy uptight losers that she dates, including the one she was crying over the night Gabe was conceived.

"Hey," Harris says.

I'm already needing to use a lot of restraint not to just plant my fist in his face. Because he says it in that super-soulful, super-personal way that makes it clear he's trying to get her to look into his eyes and hear him out. And we haven't even stepped through the door yet.

"Just can the crap and let her get her stuff," I say.

Maddie glares at me. We haven't even made it in the front door and I've already violated the agreement she and I made that I wouldn't interfere.

I shrug. I didn't actually ever intend to keep my mouth shut. I just said that so she'd take me with her.

Harris takes a step back, looking uncertain, but then he says, "I'd like a chance to talk to you, Maddie. Without—*him*."

He says it like I'm something she dragged in on her shoe, but whatever—I don't give a shit what this moron thinks of me. I just want to make sure he doesn't mess with Maddie's head. "That's not going to happen," I say.

"What are you, her bodyguard? This isn't any of your business," Harris says.

My hands clench of their own accord. Harris and I have

never exactly gotten along. We are civil to each other for Maddie's and Gabe's sakes, but you already know what I think of him, and I'm pretty sure his opinion of me is more or less what my dad's was.

I force myself to stay calm. "I beg to differ. When the mother of my kid shows up crying in the middle of the night, it becomes my business."

I don't think I've ever used that phrase before—"the mother of my kid." Maybe "baby mama" a time or two, mostly in jest. "Gabe's mom," for sure. But not *the mother of my kid.*

I didn't think it would feel so—weighty.

"There's nothing to talk about," Maddie says. "Just let me get my stuff."

Atta girl. Harris catches my triumphant smile and gives me a death-laser look, but there's not much he can do about it. He steps back and she steps in. I follow her into the condo.

It's like something you'd see in a magazine. Walls of windows, metal and black granite everywhere, built-ins. Furniture that has the clean lines of the stuff you find at Ikea but looks like it's a hell of a lot more expensive. Soulless.

Harris follows both of us down the hall and tries to cut past me to get closer to Maddie, but I edge him out. I block the door of the master bedroom and he's reduced to standing in the hallway, peering around me, watching as she pulls a suitcase from the closet and begins throwing clothes into it.

After a while, Harris drifts away. I feel victorious, although all I've done is lay claim to the doorframe. I go into the bedroom, thinking I'll sit on the bed and keep her company, but that feels too fucking weird, sitting on the bed she and Harris share. Shared. So I just watch as she fills the suitcase, trying not to stare at what she puts in there—filmy-thin nightgowns, lace panties that don't seem to contain enough fabric to cover the crucial bits, and—

She shoves the item into the suitcase before I can make out much other than a few black leather straps, but I swear it was some kind of bodysuit.

"What was that?"

"None of your business."

"Was that clothing?"

"None. Of. Your. Business."

I shut up, but not before I have time to think, *I might have to make it my business to find out what that was.*

As if she can tell that I have too much idle time to make trouble, she says, "Will you go pack Gabe's toys for me?"

Gabe's room here doesn't even feel like a kids' room. It's navy and burgundy, and all the toys and games and stuffed animals are neatly hidden away in boxes and cabinets and on shelves in the closet. It's like Maddie has been trying to make Gabe inconspicuous in Harris's life. Which makes me really mad all of a sudden. Why get yourself in a relationship with a woman who has a kid if you don't want a kid?

The whole process doesn't take nearly as long as you'd think. We're packed up within an hour and a half, nothing left of Maddie or Gabe in the condo. We've removed her from Harris's life as if she and Gabe were nothing more than a splinter under his skin.

Mia can move in this afternoon, I think bitterly, and wonder if Maddie's thinking the same. She's put on a brave face this whole day, and I'm proud of her.

Harris reappears as we're carrying boxes and suitcases down to the car.

"Maddie. Can we talk, please? Just five minutes."

I can see her resolve wavering. "You don't have to, Maddie. You don't owe him anything."

"Dude. Not your fucking business."

Harris is really pissed now, arms crossed, a storm-cloud expression on his face, which makes me happy. "Five minutes, Maddie."

"You don't deserve five minutes of her time," I tell him.

"What is your fucking problem?"

"You cheated on her."

"Jack," Maddie warns.

Harris stares at me, challenging. "Isn't that the pot calling the kettle black?"

My right fist knots, and before I can summon anything remotely resembling self-control, it has landed itself across Harris's jaw with a satisfying thud.

8

JACK

We drive to my mom's apartment—vacant while she visits her friends in San Francisco—because even though Harris for sure got the worse end of the stick, Maddie doesn't want Gabe to see me until the swelling at my cheekbone goes down a little.

I let us in with my key, and she raids the freezer and fills a zip-close baggie with ice. She finds a clean dish towel, wraps it around the bag, and presses the bundle to my cheek.

I flinch, but she doesn't ease up.

She's pissed at me. She spent most of the car ride here telling me what a colossal dick I am. She told me I'll be lucky if Harris doesn't send the cops after me. She said she's never listening to anything I say again, because I lied to her when I said I wouldn't get into it with him.

But despite all that, I'm feeling like I ran a marathon and saved a city and whatever clichés of heroism and super-heroism you can think of, because let's face it: Maddie's putting an ice pack on my face. Everyone knows the winner of the fight gets the woman with the cool hands and the first aid kit. And even though she only stopped yelling at me about thirty seconds ago, I think she's secretly pleased that I punched him. I'm sure she wanted to.

"Sit," she says, pulling out a kitchen chair. She's shorter than I am and it's awkward for her to hold the ice on my face. So I sit, and she stands next to me and leans in to examine the damage. Which isn't much, because Harris can't throw a punch worth shit.

Okay, that's a lie. Harris landed a decent blow. It hurt a lot, but it was worth it, because I heard Maddie gasp when Harris's fist made contact. I'm pretty sure she didn't gasp when my fist hit Harris's face.

Taking the punch was definitely worth it. Maddie leans closer, her breath brushing my forehead. Her teeth nibble at that incredibly sexy, full lower lip. My face is an inch from the swell of her breasts, maybe less. She's wearing a pale pink long-sleeved T-shirt made of a soft fabric that clings to her curves and leaves very little to the imagination. Definitely not the fact that her bra is made of lace. Or that her nipples are hard under the lace.

So I do what any guy would do in this situation, amped up on adrenaline and enjoying the spoils of battle: I lean forward so I can tease my lips across the tight peaks of her nipples. And when she groans, I tangle my fingers in her hair and pull her mouth down to mine so I can fully taste my victory.

She makes a small whimpering sound that burrows itself straight into my groin, and just like that, I'm hard. Harder when her mouth opens and her tongue strokes mine, harder still when she makes that noise again.

And then it's over. She pulls back and straightens up.

Her lips are already swollen, her face is flushed, and it makes me imagine how the rest of her body is responding: nipples tightening, pussy plump like her lips, the moisture pooling, ready for my touch. I reach for her again but she backs away, shaking her head.

"Jack, no."

"Maddie, *yes.*"

"No. I can't."

"Tell me you don't want it. Tell me I imagined that sexy little moan. Tell me you're not wet right now."

I apparently didn't imagine it, because she moans again. But then she takes another step away from me and says, "We can't do this."

"Why not?"

She takes a deep breath. "I'm not going to try to deny that I want it."

"Good. Because I know you do."

Her mouth softens, just enough for me to see. "Jack, you're making it worse."

"I think your 'making it worse' is my 'cutting the bullshit.'"

"Jack, I'm a mess. My life is a mess. My boyfriend cheated on me with my best friend. I just moved out. I have no place to go. I'm feeling incredibly lucky to have somewhere I can crash and someone who's in my corner. You may not want the title, but at this point you're basically my only friend in the world. And there's no way I'm going to risk that over sex."

She finishes and crosses her arms, hiding further temptation from my view.

I'm honestly speechless. I was totally prepared to run roughshod over any of her objections. And—maybe because socking Harris made me stupid and cocky—I was pretty sure I was going to win this one. I was pretty sure I'd have her kissing me again inside of five minutes, one of those tight nipples bare and caught between my fingers inside of ten.

It's that thing she does. Call it whatever you want, but she can turn me upside down faster than anyone. In this case, it was what she said about being her friend. It shouldn't have come off as anything other than pathetic. But instead it sobers me up, and it makes me remember.

It was a rainy Saturday in early December. We were eleven or twelve, and Maddie and I were playing Wiffle ball in the street with some neighborhood kids, not giving a shit that our clothes were slowly becoming soaked. There were probably eight of us, mostly boys, but a couple of girls, too.

I was pitching. Maddie was catching. I had just thrown a mean third strike past a boy named Jared when I saw my father coming up the street toward us. He was obviously looking for me, which was a bad sign. Having my father's attention turned on me was never a good thing. I tried whenever possible to stay under the radar.

It was different for Sienna. He wasn't as hard on Sienna. But when my father turned his sights on me, my first instinct was to run—or burrow into the ground.

"Jack!" he bellowed. "Jack, get your ass over here."

He was a big guy, almost two hundred pounds, barrel-chested, a little bowlegged. He was wearing a Seahawks sweatshirt and jeans. He needed a haircut and a shave.

The other kids mostly looked at the ground or at the sky

—the ones who'd never heard anyone talk to them that way —or winced sympathetically—the ones who got talked to the way my dad talked to me.

I tossed the ball to the first baseman and made my way slowly over to my father. I could see he was riled up. He was breathing hard and the color was high in his face, his eyes hard and small. He grabbed my arm, too tight.

"They just delivered the wreaths for the baseball fundraiser. And you fucked up the order. Jesus, Jack, how hard is it? All you had to do was copy the orders from the order sheets to the master sheet. Couldn't you even do that right? And now we're out sixty bucks for someone else's fucking Christmas wreaths."

"I—"

"No excuses," he said, voice hard, fingers digging into my arm. "No excuses. No apologies. You'll pay me back the sixty, and you'll call the families and explain. That you're a fucking idiot and can't transcribe numbers from one sheet of paper to another. Jesus. You are so fucking stupid."

He dropped my arm as if disgusted with it and with me, turned around, and walked back toward the house.

My face was hot. My whole body was hot, and shaking. I recognized the feeling as rage and humiliation. It was familiar. The whole scene was familiar.

The Wiffle ball game had started up again during his tirade. I think the other kids wanted to pretend it wasn't happening. Someone else was pitching now. If I'd gone back and reclaimed my spot, I'm sure they would have given it back to me, but I couldn't. I started walking away. Slowly at first, then faster, speeding up to a trot. I wanted to get far away.

I'm going to run away.

From home, I meant, but the truth was, I wanted to run away from myself, and the fact that I knew that wasn't possible made me even angrier.

"Jack."

I ignored her at first.

"Jack! Wait up."

I slowed down and let Maddie catch up. She fell in alongside me. It was like we were jogging together, only with no particular destination. We ran for a long time, the rain getting heavier, soaking our hair, rolling down our faces.

The rage softened and washed away. I was left with a numb hurt. We slowed down to a walk.

"You're *not* stupid."

She was fierce. She was almost as fierce as my father. I felt like I was caught between them, suspended between the way my father saw me and the way Maddie saw me. I teetered there.

"Yeah, well, I fucked up the order."

"People make mistakes."

I'm sure it was something her parents had said to her. It was something good parents said to their kids.

"I make a *lot* of mistakes. I don't make anything except mistakes."

"That's not true, Jack. You do the right thing a lot."

"Like when?"

We stopped and faced each other. She thought about it hard. I watched water drip off the end of her nose, which was red from the cold. She wasn't pretty yet. She was just Maddie, brown-haired and scrappy and the person I most wanted to be near.

"Do you remember the time during the lightning storm when you held my hand?"

I did. She'd been so scared she couldn't catch her breath. She'd looked like she was going to crack into a million pieces, and I'd put my hand out without thinking about it. I just *did*. And when her breathing had slowed and her face had unfrozen, I'd felt like I'd won the lottery.

It had never happened again and neither of us had ever mentioned it. Until now.

I nodded.

"Not all boys would do that. They would be awkward or whatever. But you knew I was scared, and you did the right thing. So see? You do."

She said it with so much authority that I didn't know how to argue with her. And anyway, I didn't want to argue anymore.

I wanted to be who she thought I was.

9

____

JACK

Two cool hands settle over my eyes. I smell lilac body wash, and a second later, a pair of tits whose epic proportions I'm intimately familiar with press into my back.

"Long time no see," a voice murmurs, close to my ear. "What are you doing later tonight?"

I extricate myself from the octopus that is Lani Wellings and turn around on my bar stool. I'm in O'Hannihans with Henry, Chase, and Chase's buddy Brooks, watching the dregs of a college basketball game. It's Saturday night. I offered to Maddie that if she wanted to go out, I'd stay home with Gabe, but she said she wanted to get him settled in and make sure he was okay, unpack a few basics. "Not that I'll be here long," she said quickly.

I wanted to tell her she could stay as long as she wanted, but after what had happened in my mom's kitchen this afternoon, I wasn't sure how good an idea that was.

What I should be doing is chasing the kind of no-strings

encounter that's being displayed before me: Lani in a satin bustier and a barely there miniskirt.

"Hey, Lani," I say, working the eyes-up angle with some difficulty.

"Hey, Jack, what's up? Anything for me?" She swoops a piece of raven-black hair behind an ear and grins.

Henry, Chase, and Brooks have drifted off, being too good friends to cock-block me.

Lani is slot number one on my mental speed dial, the most consistently beneficial of all my friends. She and I go way back, nearly as far back as Maddie and I. Lani is the proud possessor of my virginity, actually, though the same isn't true in reverse. She was two years ahead of me in school and may hold the distinction of having popped the cherries of more high school boys than any other girl to have graduated from Revere Lake High School.

I am momentarily tempted by the onslaught of lilac and curves—not to mention Lani's amazing mouth, which is slicked berry pink tonight. Then I remember that Maddie is sleeping in my house. It would be somewhere between awkward and impossible to bring Lani back there (we could always go to Lani's place), but that's not what ices me out. It's the fact that it's Maddie. Maddie just makes Lani seem too gaudy, too obvious, too easy. But even that's not the whole story. It's more that thinking about Maddie makes it so painfully obvious that what Lani and I do is just the sexual equivalent of scratching a mosquito bite. Vaguely satisfying, but only very briefly. And yeah, sometimes you gotta scratch, but—

"Aw, Lani, I gotta take a rain check tonight."

She pouts. "You seeing someone? It's been too long, Jack."

It has been a while, actually. And Lani's right: The only time we go this long without hooking up is when one of us is with someone else.

"No," I say. "Not seeing anyone."

Except in my midnight fantasies.

But I don't say that out loud.

She swipes a finger gently across my cheekbone. "What happened here?"

"Took a board to the face at work."

She frowned sympathetically. "How're things otherwise?"

"They're good. Gabe and Maddie are staying with me for a bit."

"Really?"

She knows the outlines of the story. Obviously, that Maddie and I hooked up, that things went south, that since then it's been somewhere between weird and outright awkward between us.

"So that's where you've been," she says, raising an eyebrow significantly.

"No. Not like that. They just needed a place to crash while they look for a new apartment."

One of Lani's most charming traits is her total lack of jealousy. Usually, I tell her pretty much everything about my sex life, and she does the same in reverse—sometimes it's even part of the game we play with each other—but tonight I'm not in the mood to share.

She shrugs. "Just be careful, Jack. Roommates are tricky. I've fucked a few too many roommates, and it never ends up well for the rent getting paid."

That makes me laugh.

"Okay," she says, laughing too. "If you're not going to ease my pain, I'm off to find someone who will."

"You do that, babe," I tell her, and she waves a chipper goodbye and sails across the room.

The guys drift back.

"A sure thing's nice," Henry says wistfully.

"She's in the market," I tell him. Getting Henry laid is a perpetual pet project of mine.

"You're not taking her home?"

I shake my head. "I've got Maddie staying with me."

"You *what*?" Henry is looking at me like I'm stark raving mad. Which maybe I am.

"She needed a place to stay," I say defensively. "Her boyfriend... dumped her."

"And you're that place?"

"She didn't really have anyone else she could ask."

I'd been about to tell the guys the whole story, about Harris and Mia, but I just don't think Maddie would want them to know. Not that she did anything wrong, but it's humiliating, still, right, being in that position? I still get pissed every time I picture her walking in on that. I drain my beer to soak the anger.

"That's going to seriously fuck up your game," Henry says.

I give him the finger. "At least I've got game."

"Past tense. You *had* game. Look at those three," he says, and gestures across the room at a stunning set—a blonde, a redhead, and a brunette, just like a bad joke. "What's your plan, man? The car? A motel? Or tell her your kid's mom is at your place but she won't mind if you two bump uglies for a bit as long as you keep the volume down? Or maybe Maddie will want to join in—"

"Don't be a dick, Henry," Chase says, and I shoot him a grateful look. Even though Chase doesn't know the whole story of what went down between me and Maddie, he knows Maddie deserves respect. "How long?"

"I don't know," I say. "She says she'll get out as soon as she finds a place."

"Just as long as this doesn't fuck up Phoenix," Henry says. The four of us have plans to head down for the March Madness championship games. Brooks has a friend who can lay his hands on tickets, which isn't the kind of opportunity that comes along every day.

"I found an Air BNB," Brooks says. "We'd each have our own room, and there's a hot tub. Nice setup, right?"

"I have to make sure Katie's nanny is good for the overnights," Chase says. "Or her grandma can take her."

I give him a look that says, *I feel you, brother.*

"Aw," says Brooks. "Look at that. It's the single dad survival club."

Neither Chase nor I denies it. It's not a bad thing, being around someone who can feel your pain.

"Don't screw up Phoenix," Henry pleads.

"Maddie'll be gone from my house by then," I say, with confidence. "She's looking at places tomorrow—"

"You watching her kid?"

"What the fuck, Henry? He's my kid, too."

Henry shrugs.

"It's not funny," I tell him.

Henry loses the smile. And stares at me, eyes narrowed, for a minute. "That bruise on your ugly mug have anything to do with her and her ex?"

I look away.

He shakes his head. "You better hope she finds another place to live fast."

Truer words have never been spoken. Just before I left to come here, Maddie asked if I'd mind keeping an eye and an ear open for Gabe, who was watching *Dora the Explorer*. She wanted to take a quick shower.

It wasn't Gabe who was the problem. He sat quietly and watched his show.

I was the problem. I couldn't stop picturing her in there. Stripping off that clingy pink top and the lacy bra I'd brushed with my lips earlier. I could see her, reflected in the mirror, nipples drawn tight, dark against the heavy globes of her breasts. The slight, soft curve of her belly and the neat triangle of reddish-brown curls between her legs. Her pale, juicy thighs, squeezed together—because in my fantasy she's thinking about me the same way I'm thinking about her.

She steps into the shower and the water is sluicing over her, trickling between her breasts, between her legs, teasing her tipped-up nipples, and I step in there with her—

And, cut.

Maddie's a good person, and no matter how things went down between us later, she deserves better than whatever it was I thought I was doing this afternoon in my mom's kitchen.

And she's right. We are friends. We got past the ugliness in our past, and the way things are now, it's more like when we were kids, before things ever got complicated. When I just knew, without it having to be said out loud, that I could count on her, and she could count on me.

She's definitely right that there aren't a whole lot of people she can say that about right now. I don't want to take that away from her. Which sex would definitely do. We know that from past experience.

We can't just screw around, then go our separate ways if things don't work out. Between the two of us, we have to make things right for Gabe.

That said, as long as Maddie is in my house, I'm going to die a little every time she changes her clothes, takes a shower, slides into bed . . .

"Amen to that, brother," I tell Henry, and order another beer.

10

MADDIE

Jack comes into the kitchen, pours himself a steaming cup of coffee, and slugs about half of it down. It makes my throat hurt, watching him. He looks pretty wiped, like he didn't sleep much, which—well, I know he didn't.

"Thank you for making coffee," he says.

"You're welcome."

He's wearing his usual morning attire, or lack thereof. It's hard to look at him and breathe at the same time, so I avert my eyes from the expanse of tanned skin and busy myself with cleaning up the dishes from Gabe's and my breakfast.

"How was your evening?"

I raise an eyebrow. "Not as much fun as yours." Then I'm annoyed with myself for letting him know that I have any idea when he came home or that I care *at all* what he was doing last night.

I didn't mean to keep tabs on him while he was out with his guy friends, but part of my brain refused to give up the ghost and go to sleep, so I know he came in around 2 a.m. I also didn't mean to spend any of the time he was gone imagining what he was doing, but I kept picturing him the way he was in high school, surrounded by girls, grinning, holding court. I could see him, older and even better looking, doing the same thing at a bar, and then going home with one of them, holding her hand, whispering something sexy in her ear as they slipped out past the other patrons.

It hurt my stomach to imagine it.

"Just beer and basketball," he says lightly. "Then a couple other guys showed up and we got into a darts tournament."

I am ridiculously relieved.

Just like last night, when I heard him come in and pad past my room to his. Relieved, and then mad at myself for feeling it.

It's clear I have to find a new place as fast as possible. Because even though I was the one who put the brakes on at Jack's mom's apartment, I don't trust myself to do it again.

As soon as he put his mouth on mine yesterday, I started wanting things. The two of us naked. The two of us wrapped around each other. And I figured that it wouldn't take long—based on previous experience—for me to start wanting the other stuff, too. The two of us snuggled up in bed. The two of us spending the whole night together. Gabe coming in to wake the two of us up in the morning. All of us living together as a family.

It was like Jack's kiss pushed a Stupid Girl button in my head that made me forget that none of that was ever going to happen. And I knew that if there was more kissing, there would also be more Stupid.

"So," I say, closing the mental door on that ache. "Janice is going to come watch Gabe so I can apartment hunt. I tried to see if she could watch him at her place, but her husband is sick in bed."

"Why'd you call Janice?" Jack asks sharply. "I can watch him."

I'm startled. "I— Honestly, it didn't even occur to—" I'm most of the way through that sentence before I think better of it, but when I meet Jack's eyes, he looks hurt. "Um, I just figured you'd be busy with stuff."

"Nothing as important as you finding an apartment," he says. "I'll watch him."

On one hand, this is a very nice thing for him to say. On the other, I feel a little pang of hurt that he obviously wants me out of here quickly.

"Are your mom and sister still out of town? You could call one of them—"

I'm trying to make it easier on him, but now he's glaring at me.

"Why, because you think I can't handle him?"

"I didn't say that."

"I watch him all the time."

Okay, Jack, enough self-righteousness. I know your game.

I give him a stern look.

"What?" Despite the tired eyes and disreputable beard shadow, he still pulls off puppy-dog innocence.

"I read your mom's Facebook account. Every time you have him, she posts photos. I know who watches him on 'your' weekends." I air-quote it.

To his credit, he drops the act with a shrug. "Yeah. Okay. So most of the time, I have help. But I did fine Friday. And you don't have to pay Janice. Save your money for first and last months' rent and security."

I'd be happy not to have to pay Janice to watch Gabe. That said, I have to do what's best for Gabe. "It'll be a long day, and he'll be awake, not like Friday night."

"Have a little faith."

He doesn't really inspire it, not looking like a hung-over college student, half-naked and scruffy, but his newfound dad bravado is pretty amusing, and part of me just wants to see if he can pull it off. "Okay. Just—text me if you need me."

He nods. "And . . . um . . ."

"Yeah?"

"I might need you to leave me a few instructions."

I try really hard to hide my smile.

And fail.

"Wipe that smirk off your face."

I stop just short of inviting him to do it.

THE FIRST APARTMENT I see is awful.

It's far from the Seattle hospital where I work. It's shabby, the kitchen circa 1960, the linoleum and paint peeling. It's tiny—just the galley kitchen, a living room, and a single bedroom. I'd have to give Gabe the bedroom and sleep on a futon or foldout in the living room. And on top of that, it's a hundred dollars more per month than I was planning on.

Still, after spending the rest of the day seeing some really trashed apartments in some really down-on-their-luck neighborhoods, and a few semi-decent apartments that are closer to a thousand dollars out of my monthly price range, I decide that I judged that first apartment prematurely. So I park my car and call the landlord back.

"Sorry, sweetheart. Just rented it. Had five applications after you saw it this morning. Gotta strike while the iron's hot."

I squeak my distress.

"Welcome to Seattle."

I don't tell him I've lived in the Seattle area my whole life. I know this isn't the Seattle I grew up with, the one that was still recovering from an economic crash, where a billboard only twenty years before had once famously joked, "Last one to leave Seattle, turn out the lights." Now it's more like trying to stuff clowns into a car, there are so many people flooding to the city to work in technology.

I sit behind the wheel of my car, sheltered from an increasingly penetrating rain, and let myself indulge in despair.

My phone buzzes.

Jack.

It's a photo of Gabe. Tucked into bed. Surrounded by his stuffed animals. Asleep. My heart goes all melty. He looks so peaceful and cozy.

Jack has been sending photos all day.

This morning, in response to my text, *Everything okay there?* he sent one of Gabe on the playground, at the top of the little-kid rock wall, holding on for dear life and grinning like a fiend.

Guess it's okay, I texted back.

Ye of little faith.

Early in the afternoon, unprovoked, he sent me one of Gabe with his face more or less planted in a ridiculously huge ice-cream cone, ice cream in his eyebrows. Shortly after that, my phone buzzed again. Gabe in the old-fashioned Revere Lake five-and-dime, holding aloft a small model car.

That place is still there?! I tapped back.

Jack and I had loved that store as kids. Because it was always full of treasures, and you never knew what you'd find. Christmas ornaments, cloth slippers, coloring books, Buddha statues, colorful plastic water guns, balloons, key chains. You could spend hours deciding how to spend a dollar. Best bang-for-the-buck around.

Still here. Not sure how, but still here.

An hour later, he sent a video of Gabe throwing a football, with the header, *Spiral!!!!!!!!!!!!!!!!!*

Um, what's a spiral?

Heathen. A spiral is how you throw a football.

Next came a photo of Gabe sleeping, and I take one more peek at it, admiring his long lashes against his fat little cheeks. Of course, I'm bummed I missed bedtime, but the photo makes me smile. Partly because photos and videos of Gabe always make me smile. But also because Jack took those photos. Gabe's *daddy* took those photos. Not his grandma or his auntie.

I warn myself: *Don't you dare feel—*

Not sure what to call it. Joyful. Hopeful. All sorts of stupid set-yourself-up-for-failure emotions. All the things I've promised myself never to feel about Jack again.

Just don't.

My phone buzzes. I snatch it off the seat. It's Jack.

Mia's here. Parked out front. I told her I'd call the police, and she called my bluff. I think she's going to camp out till you show up.

Face, meet palm.

I think about driving around until Mia gives up and goes home, but I'm just so damn tired.

I see her car as soon as I pull onto Jack's street. There's a faint light inside the car—her phone. As I pass the car, I see her face, and I'm flooded with a deep, real grief.

Mia and I have been friends since college; we met one night at a coffee shop, bonding over a shared frustration with the fact that they were out of the chocolate syrup for mochas. She convinced me to follow her to another coffee shop, and then, when there was only one table, to share it with her.

"Thanks, but—I'll just wait for a table."

I was pretty shy in those days, and she wasn't my friend "type"—she was small and sharp—her nose, her words, her voice—and she had a frantic energy about her that made me nervous. The idea of having to make small talk with someone like that—it made me want to pull the brim of my baseball cap down and hide.

She narrowed her eyes at me. "You're commitment phobic, right? I can tell. You think if you sit at my table and it's awkward you won't know how to get out of it."

"I—"

"Don't lie. I can see it all over your face. But it's not a big deal. You can just get up and go. Hell, you can say, 'This is awkward as fuck, I'm outta here,' and you won't hurt my feelings. Nothing hurts my feelings."

That was so foreign to me that my immediate impulse was to demand that she explain how that was even possible. How could you not get your feelings hurt by people? *Would she teach me?*

So I sat.

That was Mia—funny, frank, resilient—the friend I hadn't

known I needed. By the end of the evening, we were laughing so hard we couldn't catch our breath. The next fall, we moved out of the dorms and into an apartment together and remained nearly inseparable through college and after.

Over time, some of Mia rubbed off on me. I learned to let things slide off me in a way I'd never guessed I'd be able to. She had a way of reframing things so they just didn't hurt so much. That girl, the one who'd ignored me in the mess hall— it wasn't that she didn't like me. It was that she was stuck in her own head and she hadn't even seen me. That guy, the one who I flirted with every Friday for a semester without ever coaxing him into asking me out? He was so busy trying to impress his football friends that he'd let love walk right by him if it didn't look like a blond cheerleader.

It wasn't usually about me. Mia could see that, somehow.

Except this time, Mia is the one who has hurt me, and there is no one who can explain how her betrayal isn't about me.

And my feelings hurt so bad right now, it's all I can do not to turn the car around and drive away, anywhere. Instead, I park in the driveway and get out. She does the same.

"You should have called."

"You wouldn't have answered."

"There's a reason for that." I glare at her, at her short, choppy black hair and her red lipstick, her compact body in a sweater and another of her stupid long skirts.

I hated the skirts even before Harris put his head under one.

"I know what I did is the worst thing anyone can do. Ever. I know I deserve to have my pubic hairs plucked out one by one—"

I'm not even tempted to laugh. I've never been good at getting or staying angry at Mia. But this is different from any of the other fights we've ever had, like the one we had over her refusal to *ever* throw away food in the refrigerator until it was visibly unsafe, or over my tendency to crawl into my own head and ignore her when I was stressed out, instead of talking about it. This isn't a fight, really. It's—

The heavy weight in my chest is because this is the end of the line. If the coffee shop was the beginning, her skirt in my kitchen was The End.

"Please," she says, seeing, I guess, the hardness on my face. "I'm so, so sorry. And I know—I know you must be so angry, and maybe you can't ever forgive me, but you should know that if you can, ever, I am still your friend."

Her voice is shaking. I can tell she means it, every word she says.

I want to ask her so many questions. How she can have the nerve to show up here and even ask my forgiveness. Whether she's in love with Harris. If they've exchanged I-love-yous or made promises to each other. If they're going to get married. If she'll live in that condo with him, sleep in my spot in the bed.

If it creeps her out.

How she could have chosen him over me.

If I'd had the choice, I wouldn't have chosen him over her.

The thought startles me.

He wasn't worth it.

I didn't love him like that.

I meet her eyes, really, for the first time. They are bleak and dead serious.

She does.

Maybe it's not really about me.

Don't get me wrong. I'm not suddenly flooded with benevolence and forgiveness. I don't throw my arms around Mia and tell her she can have him.

What I feel is more like indifference. But it's a huge relief, the indifference. It feels like a big breath of fresh air after you've been in a toxic place.

When Harris took me aside in his condo, when I went to pick up my stuff, this is what he said:

"I know you hate me. And I deserve it. And I'm not even going to bother asking you not to hate me. But if you could find it in yourself not to hate Mia—"

Mia's expression pleads with me, now.

"I don't hate you," I say.

She makes a sound of unmistakable relief.

"I don't know if I forgive you, exactly, but I don't hate you."

"Then—are we—still friends?"

Someone snorts with laughter. It's not me, and it's *definitely* not Mia. I turn toward the house and discover that at some point, Jack has slipped outside and is standing in the shadows, arms crossed, like my silent bodyguard. I'm oddly touched—and pissed.

"Go inside," I tell him.

Surprisingly, he obeys. Or—at least, he turns and walks back toward the front door. At the last minute, though, he turns back toward us.

"You idiot," he says to Mia. "It doesn't matter if she forgives you. She'll never trust you again."

He says it so fiercely that I know—*know*—he's not just talking to her. He's talking to himself.

His eyes meet mine, and they are dark and—sad. An

expression that I don't think I've seen in Jack's eyes since he was a child, since he gained the ability to hide his emotions from everyone, even me.

Does that mean he regrets it? Losing my trust?

He drops his gaze and turns back to the door.

I'm so intent on watching him as he slips back inside that it's almost a surprise to me when Mia speaks again. Like I've forgotten she's there.

"He's right, isn't he?"

Her eyes are sorrowful, and locked on mine.

I'm so tired.

"Probably," I say, and then I turn and follow him inside.

11

JACK

I'm sitting on the couch when Maddie comes inside.

"What was that about?" she demands.

"What was what about?"

I should have kept my mouth shut. Even as the words were coming out of my mouth, *It doesn't matter if she forgives you. She'll never trust you again,* I knew she'd find a way to twist them around.

"What you said to Mia."

"Just the truth. She's an idiot to think she can steal your boyfriend and ever be your friend again."

Maddie looks like she wants to say something else, but instead she rolls her eyes at me and sits on the chair across from me. "Ain't that the truth."

"You want a beer?"

She hesitates, then nods.

I go and collect two bottles from the fridge, pop the tops, and hand her one. She takes a long swallow, and my mouth goes dry at the sight of hers wrapped around the bottle. At the long column of her throat. At the expanse of bare skin visible where her jacket and her sweater part to reveal the vee of the shirt underneath.

"Harris is right, you know," she says abruptly.

"About?"

"Pot calling the kettle black. With him, and now with Mia, too."

See, now, this, this is exactly why I should have kept my mouth shut in both cases. Because I should have known it would lead back here, back to Maddie's and my history. And that is not a place either of us needs to revisit.

"They both needed to be called out on their bullshit," I say, shrugging.

"And you don't?"

I shrug again. "Everyone does."

She raises her eyebrows and I wonder if she's about to call *me* out, but she just takes another drink of beer.

I am a tiny bit disappointed that she's going to let it go. Like part of me is hoping she'll light into me so I can—

So I can what?

Sometimes I think about bringing it up with her. Talking it through with her. But then I think, the past is past, and it wouldn't change the fundamentals of the situation. Even if I could go back and make a different decision that night, it wouldn't make me a family man. It wouldn't suddenly deliver us a happily-ever-after, because I'm not a happily-ever-after guy. It's not in the genes.

Time for a change of subject. "Did you see anything good tonight?"

She gives me this confused look, like the thing with Mia and this conversation between us made her forget completely how she spent her evening. I remind her. "Apartments?"

She sighs, her shoulders slumping. "No. Everything was total crap."

She tells me about the one halfway-decent apartment she saw and how she ended up losing it because she didn't jump on it fast enough.

"Sounds like a dump anyway. No loss."

She looks away, biting her lip. "I just don't want to be in your hair longer than I have to be. It's gotta cramp your style."

I think of Henry giving me a hard time about bringing women back here, and feel a twinge of defensiveness. She's not wrong. I have my share of one-nighters, and more than just Lani on speed dial for booty-call purposes. And since this is the twenty-first century, I'm on the end of a few speed dials myself.

Though even before I turned Lani down the other night, there have been a few times the last month or two when I've had my phone out, ready to call in a favor-with-benefits, and just—stopped. Just stuffed the phone back in my pocket and taken care of business myself.

Which is a whole different thing with Maddie asleep (or maybe lying awake) down the hall . . . The last two nights when I've given in to the urge to wrap my fist around myself, I've tried to keep my mind from straying into her room, from crawling under the covers with her—but I'm not having much luck.

It's not the lack of one-nights and booty calls that's going to kill me. It's the temptation under my own roof.

As if to illustrate the point, she licks a drop of beer off the rim of her bottle, and I feel it like her tongue's on me.

Steady, Jack.

What was the logic we arrived at yesterday for why we shouldn't fuck each other into next week? It has officially fled my mind.

"You're not cramping my style."

If you'd like, I could show you a thing or two about my style . . .

"Not yet." She sighs again. "I'm going to look again tomorrow night. The sooner I find something, the sooner I can get out of your space." She takes her phone out. "I have to figure out timing tomorrow. I think I need Janice at six a.m. She's gonna hate me."

"At six, why?"

"That's when I have to leave for work."

I grimace. She twists her mouth wryly and nods. "Seven to three thirty, Monday through Friday."

Plus every third weekend. That part I know by heart. This one coming up is her work weekend, my usual weekend with Gabe.

Gabe's usual weekend with his auntie and grandmother, that is. Gotta own that. Except it was really fun being with him today. I took him the same places my mom and Sienna take him—the playground, the ice-cream parlor, the five-and-ten—but it was different when it was just him and me. Like we were just pal-ing around, hanging out.

He's actually pretty easy, now. Like, almost a person.

"I can watch Gabe in the morning until I have to leave. At seven forty-five," I say.

She looks like it's on her mind to say something disbelieving, but we went through that drill yesterday when I offered to watch him today, and all she says is, "If you're sure?"

"I don't mind."

I half expect her to refuse, but she doesn't. She just says, "You can put a show on TV for him when you need to take a shower."

"Sure."

I watch as she texts Janice, her long, slim fingers tapping, her curved fingernails making a slightly hollow sound.

"I'll be back from work by four thirty, so I'll take over from Janice then."

"I'm back around six," I say.

Then we sit for a minute, drinking our beers.

She's curled up on the couch now, tucked into the corner with the extra cushions Sienna insisted on buying for me, even though I can't see the point. Maddie's got one elbow draped over the back of the couch and her knees pulled up. As I watch, she sighs and sinks a little deeper down, like she's letting go of the day's stress—the failed apartment hunt and the confrontation with Mia. I feel some of the tension go out of me, too.

It's—oh, fuck—kind of cozy.

MONDAY MORNING, Maddie gets up, hustles herself out of the house, and leaves Gabe behind with me. I take him out to breakfast. Work is sucking hard right now and I need all the fuel I can get.

I sit him next to me at the Blue Plate Special counter, where he dangles his legs and eats a gigantic waffle with syrup and butter. I have the farmer's breakfast. Three eggs, bacon, hash browns, pancakes, toast, coffee, and OJ.

We sit side by side in companionable silence, except

when he needs me to cut more waffle pieces or pour more syrup for him.

It's pretty great.

Then Janice takes over and I head to work, feeling like the best part of my day might already be behind me.

When I get home, Maddie approaches me to say she's thinking of heading into the city, and to ask about me watching Gabe. This time, she doesn't bring up the idea of having Janice sit for Gabe, but she also doesn't just assume I'll do it, which is cool. "I know it's not your time with him and I don't want you to feel like I'm assuming I can dump him on you whenever, or like you giving us a place to crash suddenly means all kinds of responsibilities you didn't sign on for—"

"Shh."

Her eyes widen and her mouth opens. "Did you just *shh* me?"

"You're the one who always says it isn't babysitting if it's your own kid."

Her eyes narrow. "Even if you're super nice, I'm not going to change my mind about sleeping with you," she says sternly.

Oh, yeah? Not that that's why I was doing it, but now that you've made it a challenge . . . "You think pretty highly of your appeal, huh?"

"You weren't complaining the other night," she says, just as snappy, and like that, the atmosphere shifts, all the electric charges in the room lining up around us. I can't take my eyes off the dare in her eyes.

Then she drops her gaze and takes a step back.

"I shouldn't have said that. It was—"

"True?"

Her eyes are sharp, searching my face. If I didn't know her better, I'd have said uncertain, maybe even hopeful.

"Maddie—"

"Don't."

I almost tell her. That I haven't really slept since she moved in, because I'm lying awake thinking of her down the hall, wondering whether she's awake or asleep, happy or heartbroken, or—like me—horny as fuck and easing a hand down to soothe away a completely different kind of ache. I want to tell her I keep remembering things about her—the way her eyes go soft when she's aroused, the way her chest flushes when she gets close, the way her lips part right before she cries out. That I've pictured her in every stage of undress, wearing every article of clothing I know she owns and a few I'd like to buy her.

But I don't. She asked me not to.

"I'll watch Gabe as many nights as you need me to, okay? And you won't owe me anything. Hell, you carried him around for nine months and nursed him, right? I probably can't ever make that up to you."

The weird thing is, I mean it. The nine months she was carrying Gabe around, I never gave it a thought. Because she was the one who was sure she wanted to raise him, and I'd been honest with her that I didn't think I'd be any good at being a dad. I never felt guilty about her doing the work when he was a newborn or an infant—it was work she'd signed on for, and I hadn't. And it isn't like I feel guilty now, either, just—aware. Maybe it's what happened to her with Mia and Harris being such a bum deal. A pity thing. But whatever. For whatever reason, I'm conscious that she's worked hard, and it suddenly seems fair that I take a turn.

Short version: I say yes to watching Gabe Monday night. And Tuesday night. And, when the first two nights of hunting fail to turn up a decent apartment, Wednesday night.

My sister helps—she's back from her business trip, and she wants to bring dinner by and hang with Gabe. Monday and Tuesday nights, Sienna does bedtime—the tooth brushing, the reading and tucking, the trips back down the hall to get Gabe settled. She wants the time with Gabe, and I'm too fried from work to fight her.

But tonight, Wednesday night, Gabe says, "I want Daddy to do bedtime."

Sienna looks startled. She's standing beside him and I'm on the couch, drinking a beer and watching a sportscast. "I think Daddy's busy," Sienna tells Gabe, and takes his hand.

I lurch to my feet, setting my beer on the end table. "Nah. I got it."

"You need—some—help?" There is confusion written all over my sister's pretty face.

"I can do it," I tell her.

"Since when?"

I can't blame her for doubting me, but I need her to see that I'm stepping up.

"Look," I say. "I know you and Mom usually do most of the work— Did you just snort at me?"

She smirks. "Did you just say 'most of the work'?"

"Okay, I've been a slacker—stop making that face. I want to do better."

That silences her for a moment. Then she says, "Have at it."

When I come back down the hall after tucking him in, she says, "He'll be back out."

I grin. "Don't think so."

"What'd you do?"

"I tranquilized him."

The look of alarm that crosses her face would be funny if it wasn't so clear that my sister is pretty sure there is no way I can get my own kid to bed without drugging him.

I shrug. "He likes to listen to sports on the radio. I used to do it when I was a kid."

"Doesn't that keep him up?"

"Nah. Go check it out."

She goes down the hall and comes back with a sappy smile on her face. "Out cold."

I grin. "Toldja."

"So—don't hate me, but what's the deal?"

"The deal?"

"With you manning up so hard with Gabe. Does this have anything to do with Maddie hanging around?"

"Nah. Just getting my feet under me, I guess."

"Are you sure?"

She's looking at me, all concerned.

"Yeah, I'm sure."

"Because I don't want you to get hurt."

"Why would I get hurt?"

"She's living in your house, Jack. You really think that's not going to end badly?"

"Badly how?"

"With you two hooking up and you getting hurt?"

I don't answer the question. Instead I say, "I'm not the one who gets hurt when Maddie and I hook up."

She gives me a long, hard look.

And it occurs to me that just because I fed Sienna the same story about how things went down with Maddie that I fed everyone else doesn't mean she actually believes it.

12

MADDIE

You know how sometimes you're doing something, and as you're doing it there is this little part of your brain very quietly saying, *This is a horrible idea,* but you ignore it, for whatever reason?

Yeah. So, on Friday night, when I can't deal with one more night of banging my head against the apartment hunt, Gabe and I cook dinner for Jack.

I actually go to the hardware store and buy a step stool so Gabe can stand on it and "cook" with me. Obviously he's too young to chop vegetables or cut meat, so I put him to work on stuff he can handle. I carefully wash a pair of his kid scissors and have him chop parsley, and when he's done with that, I let him tear the lettuce into pieces for the salad. He thinks it's pretty much the coolest job ever. And then he arranges the grape tomatoes and cucumber slices and carrot shavings on top of the salad, and it's such a precision operation that I almost die of cuteness and have to take a video for Jack.

Meanwhile I've been making chili, and the whole kitchen smells unbelievably good, the rich, dark smell of beef and tomato sauce and the bright, leafy tang of the parsley, and that warm yellow smell of just-out-of-the-oven cornbread set on the counter to cool.

Gabe and I set the table, and everything is ready to go when we hear Jack's truck in the driveway. Gabe is jumping up and down, he's so excited to show his dad everything he's done—

So you can see where this is going, probably.

I will say, I tried to keep the expectations under control. I said, "Gabe, Daddy might not be hungry for dinner, so if it's just you and me, that's okay, too."

I tried to keep my own expectations under control, too. I told myself I was cooking for Jack to thank him for letting us stay, to thank him for watching Gabe so I could house hunt. I didn't need him to sit and eat with us; if he was busy or had other plans, the chili would keep for reheating later, maybe for lunch tomorrow or dinner some night this week. I told myself I was cooking for Jack the same way you cook for anyone you cook for—someone who's had a baby or is sick, someone who you need to thank for cat-sitting while you're on vacation, whatever.

I was very successful at convincing myself.

The front door opens and Jack's work-booted footsteps sound in the living room, and I feel my own chest expand with anticipation—

He appears in the doorway to the kitchen and I can see right away that I've barked up the wrong tree. His face is dark and shuttered, his body language closed and remote.

"You cooked." His tone holds about as much pleasure as if he were saying, "You ran over my dog with your car."

"Yeah."

"We made chili! And a salad! Look at my salad!" Gabe, oblivious to adult emotion, can barely contain himself.

"Sorry—I should have texted. I'm going out with the guys."

His voice is so hard and dismissive, I barely recognize it.

He turns away, down the hall, and I hear a door shut and then the shower running.

"He's not going to eat with us?" Gabe asks.

"I—"

I tell myself that all my anger and hurt is for Gabe and his disappointed expectations. That I don't give a shit, for all the reasons I established in my head as I was cooking. But I am really angry and hurt for Gabe. Enough that I leave Gabe in the kitchen and go down the hall and knock on the bathroom door.

"Yeah?"

Jack's voice is tight.

"There's enough—if the guys want to come over—"

I tell myself this isn't pathetic, because I'm doing it for Gabe.

There's only silence, and I think about repeating myself— it's so hard to hear someone when you're in the shower and the person is talking to you from other side of the door. I think about opening the door and speaking through the crack to him, but there's something about not having a closed door between me and naked Jack with water running down all over his body that doesn't seem like a good idea, and I've used up all my free passes for stupid ideas already today, so I don't do it.

It's not like Jack and I haven't shared meals since Gabe was born. Of course we have. Takeout after Gabe's baby and toddler birthday parties when everyone was too exhausted to contemplate cooking for the remaining assembled family members; the occasional Easter or Thanksgiving or Christmas meal when circumstances pushed us together; even, once or twice, a "hey, stay, I've got enough leftovers for an army" at a drop-off or pickup. But all those occasions were different. Most of the time, we were surrounded by other family. We were together at an event; our togetherness wasn't the event. Or the circumstances arose spontaneously and felt casual, so a "no thanks, I've gotta head back" didn't feel like a slap in the face.

I should have known better.

Jack had one purpose in my life: giving me Gabe. If he has offered his house to us now, it isn't because he wants to take care of me; it's because he feels obligated to take care of Gabe. So I shouldn't be trying to take care of him in return, no matter what my motives are.

Standing alone in the hallway, Jack on the other side of the door in whatever awful mood has overtaken him, I feel my face flush with shame. Because no matter how good a job I'd done earlier of lying to myself about not caring whether Jack ate with us or not, it was pretty clear now that I care. I care a lot.

Way too freaking much.

13

JACK

I like to think I learned something from my asshole father: that I know myself well enough not to impose my shittiness on other people, the way he did. So my plan was, I was going to take my assholic mood and drink it into oblivion in the company of Henry, Chase, and Brooks. I wasn't going to subject Maddie or Gabe to it.

My mood wasn't Maddie or Gabe's fault, not even the slightest. It was shit happening at work again. For the, I don't know, tenth time in as many days, the rich, entitled clients had changed their tune—this time about the flooring materials. And once again my crappy boss made my crew scapegoats so he could look good to his bosses at the greedy out-of-town building company that employs all of us. The whole thing is such a fucking land grab—building cheap houses out of the lowest-grade materials, not even trying to make them blend in with the vibe of the town or Revere Lake's existing housing stock, and selling them for outrageous prices to people who don't know better. I'm so tired of being part of it.

That's what had me so ballistic when I walked through the door.

But I hadn't expected Maddie and Gabe to have cooked for me. I didn't count on coming home and having Gabe bouncing up and down because he was so excited that he'd made me dinner.

Their excitement and the expectation on their faces made the way I felt instantly worse. So much worse. Because I had all this twisted, balled-up anger inside me, and it didn't think Gabe was cute or Maddie was amazing for having cooked. Instead, when I walked into my house and saw them there, I just felt like they'd invaded my space and I wanted it back. Gabe's antics were annoying and the look on Maddie's face, like I'd kicked her puppy, amped up my need to lash out. And all I could think about was my father, and how this was what he felt when he walked in the door and saw me. Another irritant in a world of things that failed to live up to his expectations.

So I got the hell out of there and into the shower. Then she followed me down the hall and tried to talk to me through the door, offering to have Henry and the guys over for dinner, as if that would solve everything.

I can't take it. I'm ready to haul off and shout at her to get out of my hair, to give me some space. The words are choked up in my throat, harsh, ready to be hurled, and the only thing I can do is clamp my mouth shut around them. I stand there, under the shower, not yelling.

The water is too hot, but I let it punish me.

What I want, what I really want, is for her to crack the door, slip in, take her clothes off, get in here with me, and let me bury my frustration in her body.

After a while I hear her retreat down the hallway, and I take a breath, and the band around my chest loosens. I think I'm gonna be okay.

I soap myself fast, roughly, and get out of the shower as fast as I can. I don't deserve to lounge around enjoying it. I definitely don't deserve to jerk off to the hot, fast arousal that crashed down on me when I imagined her in here with me.

I dress slowly. I guess I'm dragging my feet.

When I go out into the kitchen, they're sitting there, eating together, and they both look defeated. And something shifts and settles in my chest. I don't make a conscious decision or anything. I just—I sit. I pull out a chair and sit down at the third place they've set and haven't cleared.

"Daddy! Are you going to eat wid us?"

I nod.

Gabe's face lights up like you wouldn't believe.

It feels—

It feels good, and scary, too. Like, I have this power over this little person. I have the power to ruin or make his day. I have the power to teach him to be a strong, generous man or to turn him into the next generation of fucked-up Parker males in line for my dad's legacy.

And I have no idea how to do it right, you know?

Then I look over at Maddie and while she looks a little more cautious than Gabe, I can see that something has softened in her face, too. There's a smile teasing around the corner of her mouth.

(I'd like to tease around the corner of that mouth.)

(*Nope. Nope. Nope.*)

And that smile is scary, too. Because it tells me I have some power over her, too, and—

Well, that's the last thing I ever wanted.

She spoons some chili into a bowl, balances a hunk of cornbread beside it, sets a plate of salad at the corner of my placemat.

My stomach growls. It smells amazing. I dig in and let myself enjoy the situation. Home cooking, sexy woman in my kitchen, even if I can't feast on her the way I can on what's in front of me.

"You want a beer?" she asks, getting up.

"Sure."

She crosses the kitchen to the fridge and comes back with two bottles and a church key. She has her long hair pulled up in some kind of hair clip, but strands of it have gotten loose and are curling up around her face. Her makeup is smudged from a day of work, but it looks good that way, her eyes dark-rimmed and ultra-green. She's still wearing work clothes—a pretty cranberry-colored blouse tucked into light gray pants that hug her ass like a glove. And she's barefoot.

I am a fucking caveman, but I love those bare feet on my kitchen floor.

She hands me the bottles and the key and I pop one for each of us and tap my bottle against hers in a makeshift toast. Gabe wants to clink, too. He runs to the cabinet, finds a plastic cup, and asks for it to be filled with water so he can join in. The three of us do "cheers"—"chee-ahs!" in Gabe's case—and then I enjoy the first cold swallow.

Cold beer. Hot, spicy chili with hunks of tender beef and kidney beans. And this cornbread with honey that's—

There are no words.

I do, however, try to hold back the actual grunts of pleasure. I'm not a total caveman.

14

MADDIE

I come back down the hall from putting Gabe to bed. I hear the water running in the kitchen, stick my head in, and discover Jack doing the dishes.

"You're still here," I say, surprised.

"There were dishes," he says, like the fact that he's elbow-deep in suds follows obviously from that fact.

"I would have done them."

He gives me a stern look. "No way. Haven't you heard of the Federal I-Cook-You-Clean Act?" He raises an eyebrow. "Huh. What kind of asshole were you living with, anyway?"

This time, it doesn't tick me off, Jack's badmouthing Harris. After all, he was right about him, wasn't he?

"Why'd you always call him Big Dick?"

"I was wrong to do that," Jack says earnestly.

Now it's my turn to raise my eyebrows.

"He obviously has a really, really tiny dick, which makes him feel like he has to prove something by sleeping with multiple women, because if he were at all normal sized, he wouldn't have fucked things up with the hottest woman alive."

I try not to let Jack's ridiculous flattery go to my head. I know he talks like this to every woman—every one he's hitting on, anyway. Any guy can do the dishes a time or two to get in your pants; any guy can tell you you're the hottest thing on earth. None of that tells you he's going to do the dishes when you've been together for months or years, or stick around when things get tough or complicated.

You have to trust the historical evidence that he's not.

"But since you asked: I called him Big Dick because that is the only possible reason you could have *ever* decided he was worth the time of day."

I actually giggle a little. Because there's nothing better, when you're down, than having someone kick the guy who put you there in the balls.

"Hey," I say. "It was nice of you to stay for dinner. I think Gabe really appreciated it."

He rinses the soap off the last pot, sets it into the dish drainer, and turns to me.

"Gabe did, huh?" He smirks.

"And I did, too, of course. It made Gabe's day."

"I didn't stay for Gabe."

All of a sudden the kitchen feels really, really small. It's easy to forget how big Jack is, how much space he takes up—and how he can take up way more than his fair share when he looks at me like this. Serious, full of intent.

"You cooked for me. Least I could do was eat it."

So, yeah, not what I thought he was going to say. I try not to let my disappointment show. I try, more specifically, not to actually feel my disappointment. Instead, I deflect.

"What was up with you? When you got home?"

"Oh," he says. "That." He wipes around the edge of the sink and sets the sponge down.

"Yeah, that. Something happen at work?"

He shrugs.

I raise my eyebrows.

He sighs. "Work sucks right now."

"You want to tell me about it? If you've got time. I know you have to meet the guys."

"Actually, I told them I'd catch up with them later this week. I thought we could watch a movie or something."

Everything freezes in me.

"Um . . ."

"But if you don't want to, I could still head out with them. No biggie." He shrugs.

I take a deep breath. He's not asking me on a date. He's asking me to kill some evening time by sitting on opposite ends of the same couch and watching Netflix. No need to get silly about it. "No, that would be fun."

"Cool."

He busies himself wiping down the chili spatters on the stovetop. I'm staring at his back, wanting—well, what I always want. More Jack.

"Tell me about work. If you want."

I don't actually expect him to, so I'm surprised when he starts to talk, still facing away from me.

"It's just stupid, fucked-up shit. It's a clusterfuck to begin with because they're building the little pig's straw house—only uglier—but then on top of that, it's all mismanaged. So, like, there should be sign-off on everything, and paperwork on what we agreed to with the client, but there's nothing."

He sets the sponge down and turns to face me. There's a furrow between his brows and a knot at his jaw. "The project director is an asshole, the project supervisor can't manage his way out of a paper bag—not the project, not the men. He's always yelling at guys, telling them what they're doing wrong, never saying when someone's doing it right. And when anything goes wrong, the blame flows straight downhill. So morale is shit, turnover's huge—I could do either of those jobs better with my hands tied behind my back and a gag stuffed in my mouth."

"How do you know all that? About how to do it right?"

"I've been doing this since high school summers, more than ten years. I've been on a lot of projects, and I've seen them done right and I've seen them done wrong. Mostly wrong. And more and more fucked up lately. Because every-one's trying to build faster and cheaper, and there aren't enough good crews to go around, but no one bothers to train up anyone because it takes time. And they cut corners on the stuff that really matters, like safety and getting client buy-in, which isn't a way to save money or time. It costs everyone more in the end."

He's all riled up, eyes fierce. Up until that moment, I'd thought building houses was just a job for him. But now I see it. He *loves* it. And Jack on fire like this is the sexiest man on earth.

"You should do it," I say.

"What?"

"Start your own contracting business. Run it right."

I've always thought Jack would do a great job with his own business. People love him, and he's got that great combination of authority and the kind of charisma that makes people actually want to do what he asks.

He shakes his head, hard. "Nah. Whatever. I shouldn't have said that. I can't do what the boss man does. That's not my strength. I'm good with my hands."

He waggles his eyebrow at me.

I feel a surge of heat, even though I know he's trying to distract me from what he said. Because what he said is so Jack.

"You underestimate yourself," I say, pushing away the distraction. "You could do it. If you set your mind to it."

"Whatever." He waves a hand, dismissing it.

"You know what this is about?" I feel a little reckless. Maybe it's because the whole night has been so weird, like a roller coaster—all the push and pull. So it doesn't feel so risky, right now, to get a little real, get back to the way we used to be, when we talked about stuff that mattered. "This is about you thinking you're not smart enough to do it. But that's bullshit. The only reason you think you aren't is because you grew up being told over and over you weren't. But it's not true."

His face tightens. Actually, all his body language does. And I know I've gone too far. Even though I was there, so many times, when his father told him he was stupid and worthless, even though I used to be able to reassure him that he wasn't.

"You think because you knew me when I was twelve that you know who I am now?"

His jaw is tight, his eyes cold, the words hard and dagger sharp. I have to catch my breath against the stab. Because it's a fair question.

"No." I shake my head.

"A lot has changed since then."

"I know," I say. "I'm sorry—I shouldn't have—"

"Our lives went in totally different directions." He illustrates this with a gesture that makes my heart hurt—one hand rising, the other falling, the fortunes of our two families.

Not totally different, I want to say.

I'm thinking of Gabe down the hall, but also the reason that Gabe is with us, that strange night of intersection, and all the junctures before and after that hold our lives together. Jack and I are bound together, and even though in a lot of ways it makes no sense at all, in other ways, it is the most logical thing in the world.

15

MADDIE

Five years ago

I was convinced that the heartbreak I felt at age twenty-one was the most acute pain it was possible for anyone to feel. I had planned my whole life with Brian Torrence—how we were going to graduate from college and move in together in Seattle, get jobs, live together a year or two, get engaged, get married, have kids . . . and I'd been sure he was spinning exactly the same narrative in his own head.

And then three and a half weeks before we were supposed to go back to college for senior year, he came to visit me at home and told me he was breaking things off between us. He wanted to date other girls before college ended, because it might be his last chance to have such a big pool of women to choose from, and he wasn't sure enough that I was his destiny to gamble on it.

I think breakups are disappointing partly because they reveal that you never really knew the other person, or the relationship, the way you thought you did. I thought Brian was a romantic, but he was a pragmatist. I thought I was his soul mate, not a statistical probability.

(Although note: I said I thought I was his soul mate, not that he was mine. I might not have admitted it to myself, but part of me knew that the job of being my soul mate had been taken for a long, long time.)

Anyway, I was wrong about Brian and suffering from what felt like a broken heart.

Mia had come home with me for the last month of summer because her own family was traveling in Europe and she hadn't wanted to tag along. When I dumped the tear-stained story of Brian's visit on her, she insisted that we drown my sorrows in alcohol and casual sex, that I have at least one suitable rebound before I had to go back to college and watch Brian spin the slot machine.

It was summer in Revere Lake and I'd lost touch with most of the kids I'd known in high school, but Mia made me go on Facebook and friend all my high school acquaintances. As usual, her strategy was brilliant. Everyone accepted my friend request, and several different people suggested I come down to the private lake beach for an end-of-summer swim party happening that night. I asked if Mia could tag along and they all said yes and then friended her, too.

So we shaved and waxed, painted our finger- and toenails, and did each other's hair. We pulled out our sexiest bathing suits and cover-ups and high-heeled sandals, and we showed up at the private beach club on Revere Lake in the evening with six-packs in all four hands and mysterious, sexy smiles on our faces. We drank too much and we flirted crazily and we swam in our skimpy bikinis and then stood in the cooling air, knowing our nipples were visible and the goosebumps rippling over our skin were a taunt to the opposite sex. Or I did all that, anyway.

I knew Jack Parker was there. I always knew when Jack Parker was anywhere near. I could feel him like the near-brush of a hand that lifts the peach fuzz on your skin.

He was standing by the boathouse, surrounded by women. He'd had a reputation all through high school for being something of a sex god, a reputation that was said to be well deserved.

Our families' fortunes had—exactly as Jack said in the kitchen—diverged. When Jack's father left his family, emptied the bank accounts, and disappeared, Jack's mother went into a tailspin, had a nervous breakdown, and lost her job and—eventually—their house to foreclosure. After a year or so, she pulled herself together, and she and Jack both worked jobs and kept the family together, but they were always barely hanging on. And that was how Jack was, too—barely hanging on to staying in school, to staying out of jail. Narrowly avoiding getting anyone pregnant or crashing his car or ending up addicted to something dangerous.

I watched all of it from a distance, because Jack and I weren't friends anymore. We'd ruined our friendship years ago, and I didn't know how to fix it. It was a kiss—of course. Even at not-quite-thirteen, I understood that kissing ruins friendships.

We'd been playing a neighborhood game of sardines and I'd found him crouched on the stairs under his basement's bulkhead. I snuck in next to him and he quickly pulled the door closed and plunged us into darkness. In the gloom under the bulkhead, Jack whispered to me that his parents had fought so loud the night before that he couldn't sleep, and I whispered back, "That *sucks.*"

It was the first time Jack and I had been in the dark since the thunderstorm, more than two years earlier, and all of a sudden I remembered what it had felt like when Jack held my hand, and I got this craving for him to do it again. My mouth felt dry and my hands prickled. And then, as if I'd made him do it by sheer force of will, I felt his hand around mine again. Big. Warm. And that sense of comfort flowing into me. Only in that situation, because I didn't need comfort to start out with, it was like with all of Jack's warmth flowing into me, there was too much to contain. I felt like I was going to overflow with it. It needed to go somewhere. I turned my face toward Jack, mostly to see if he was as freaked out by this as I was, if he was also having a problem with the comfort feeling being too much for his skin, and my nose bumped his nose and his lips touched mine. A sigh of relief slipped from my mouth, because it was exactly right.

And it felt so good.

A second later we heard voices and the clang of the bulkhead being breached, and we jumped apart.

The next day, he avoided me.

At first, I was grateful, because I needed some time to think, but then it was a week, and then almost a month, and I knew: He wasn't going to kiss me again. Then my mom told me that Jack's father had left, and that made it so much worse because something terrible had happened and Jack hadn't wanted to tell me.

We were not-friends for the rest of eighth grade and all of high school and my first few years of college. But not-friends in a very specific way. We'd walk down the hall in school and pass each other and not look at each other, but I knew exactly where he was.

I wondered if he knew exactly where I was. It felt like he did when he passed me in the hallway. Like he was not-looking at me, not being my friend, with as much energy and precision as I was not-looking at him and not being his friend.

We moved in increasingly different circles, his consumed with getting high, getting laid, and getting jobs; mine with getting into college and getting out of town.

Jack didn't go to college; he stayed in Revere Lake and worked construction. He cleaned his act up somewhat over time, bought his mom a house, and became more or less an upstanding citizen, but he was definitely still continuing to mine the depths of the local female population, according to rumor.

I was too mature, too self-assured, too smart, too driven to get anywhere near someone like Jack Parker, even if I still remembered—and sometimes longed for—a different Jack Parker. A gentle boy.

Except that night at the lake, after Brian dumped me, I wasn't any of those things—mature, self-assured, or smart.

Dark was falling and I was tipsy and getting maudlin, and Mia was having a vivacious, hilarious conversation with a guy named Eaton, and I wandered down along the shore a ways and stared out over the water and started to cry.

Not hard. Not sobs or anything. Just tears running down my face, because I'd had everything perfectly planned with Brian and now none of it was going to happen.

I thought I was alone and I thought it was too dark for

anyone to see even if someone had been there, but then I heard a voice.

"Are you crying?"

"No," I said reflexively, and turned to find Jack Parker walking along the shore toward me.

"You *are* crying."

"I'm not."

"You are."

It was so absurd that I actually laughed, which in turn made me sob for real, and then I was crying in earnest, hard.

"Oh, Jesus, what the fuck?"

"I'm sorry!"

"Just—what?"

"Bad breakup," I said breathlessly, shuddering, gesturing with one hand that he should go.

But he didn't. He stepped closer, touched my hair. "Hey," he said, his voice surprisingly gentle.

The intimacy was totally inappropriate, except it wasn't. Because I still remembered him holding my hand during thunderstorms and kissing me in a dark basement during a game of sardines—the last time he touched me before he stopped talking to me permanently. *The last time he'd touched me.*

His hand moved over my hair, barely touching, setting up a firestorm of tingles all over my scalp. My whole body.

"Don't cry," he said. "I never liked it when you cried."

It was the first time we'd exchanged words of any kind since the day he'd kissed me in the dark, and to hear our friendship referred to as something that had actually happened was overwhelming. I often feared that I'd dreamed it—our games of Stratego, our rambunctious outdoor play, our serious conversations, the hand-holding, the single kiss that had heralded the end of all of it—and to have him confirm it made me instantly warm and pliable. So when he drew me into his arms, I went, with no resistance at all.

Sound familiar?

He was warm and strong, every muscle toned and strung against me—his abs through his T-shirt against the softer curve of my bare belly, his thighs pressing against mine, his arms wrapped like cords around me. I could feel his breath moving against my hair, still setting up those tingles, those waves of shimmery warmth.

And, yeah, making itself known between us, Jack's arousal, increasingly insistent, the inverse of my own hollow want.

Step away.

Just take a step back. Thank him for comforting you, and walk away.

Instead, I tilted my chin up so I was looking into his eyes. They were dark and needy and confused, and I couldn't look away. It was as if time had fallen away and we were back under that bulkhead in the dark alone, and I was waiting for the inevitable.

His lips on mine.

And then they were there, soft but assured, then harder, insistent, then almost rough as he fisted my damp hair and pressed himself against my hip and fitted me to him.

"You're a better kisser than you were when we were kids," he said against my ear a moment later, clutching me to him as we both panted.

"So are you."

He kissed me again, bit my lip. I yelped. Then he bit it

again and licked the spot he'd bitten. The scrap of fabric between my legs was damp, and not from lake water. He confirmed this with a hand that slid down my bare belly and into my bikini bottom without waiting for permission. He groaned quietly. He looked up, as if remembering for the first time that we were more or less in public—too far from the mob to be obvious, but definitely within visual range.

"Follow me," he said, tugging a little on my arm.

"Where?"

"There's another boathouse, a little ways . . ."

I should tell Mia.

I shouldn't go.

I need to walk away. Now.

I made a decision.

He led me over the sand, through a short stand of trees, and sure enough there was another structure there, just out of view. He got me inside the door before he began kissing me again and pressed me hard against the wall, pinning me with his hips so I could barely wriggle enough to get the friction I now desperately needed. I was so elated to be kissing Jack Parker I could barely stand it. He smelled like himself, like clean soap and the indefinable scent of his skin, and like lake water and beer, and I was lapping it up, all of it, my tongue sliding along his, unstoppable, my whimpers and moans caught in his mouth. I was writhing in his arms, that's how turned on I was.

"You're so fucking hot," he said. "I knew you would be. I dreamed you just like this."

Which was funny to me because I'd never been like this before with anyone, so for him to have dreamed me like this when I didn't even know I had it in me—how did that make any sense?

I was the one who slid his swim trunks down and wrapped my hand around him, satisfyingly, hugely, Jack. I was the one who pulled at the ties behind my neck so he could get his mouth on my nipples, the one who wriggled my bikini bottom down.

He was the one who hoisted me against the boathouse wall and—hesitating only long enough to ask if I was on the Pill and to promise me he'd never in his life had sex without a condom—took me in a single, deep thrust that—swear to God—made me come, with huge, convulsive, grabby spasms that I could feel everywhere.

He covered my mouth with his hand so people wouldn't hear us all the way back at the beach and fucked me until he came, rigid, head thrown back and mouth open in a silent, triumphant shout.

16

———————

JACK

I t's not that I'm mad at Maddie for trying to convince me that I'm smarter than I think I am. It's that I just don't understand what she expects of me. Maybe I'm not a lost cause, but I'm not the kind of guy she thinks I am, either. I'm not the guy who's going to start his own business and grow it into an empire and live in one of the big houses he built. I'm just Jack, and I'm sorry if that's a disappointment to her, but that's how it is.

So I do what any guy would do in my shoes. I change the subject. "You pick the genre. And I'll pick the movie. Or the other way around. I pick the genre, you pick the movie."

She nods. I'm not sure what the look on her face is. I think I've made her feel bad, which was sort of what I set out to do, but now I'm not sure it was really what I wanted to do. What I wanted to do was say, *Thank you. For bothering to hold onto your faith in me even though I didn't earn it.*

But then I remember that in the end, she didn't. Not really. Not when it mattered.

"*You* pick the genre," she says.

"Sports."

She rolls her eyes, thinks for a minute, then smiles slyly. When she smiles like that, I want to kiss the smile off her face. "*Bend It Like Beckham.*"

She was the one who originally made me watch that movie, so she's pretty much just messing with me. "That's not a sports movie."

She gives me a look. "You made the rules."

"Okay, okay."

We find it on Netflix and camp out on the couch. She's at one end, I'm at the other, with acres of room between us. I can't help being disappointed. "Accidental" contact during movies is something I will probably still be chasing even when I am crushing on some ninety-year-old lady in the nursing home.

"You mind if I—?" she asks, around the time Jess lies to Joe and tells him her parents know she's been playing soccer. As she asks it, she hoists her feet up onto the couch, with her knees up so she's still not touching me.

A little later I feel the bottoms of her feet against my thigh, and a little after that, I scoop her feet up and rest them on my thigh, and then, because that's actually kind of painful, her heels digging into the muscle, I slide toward her and loop her legs over mine so if I wanted to, I could rest my crossed arms on her knees.

As Jules catches Joe and Jess leaning into their first kiss, I start watching Maddie instead of the movie. She's just so— into it. Big-eyed, emotions moving over her face, mouth parting and closing as if she's about to kiss, about to speak. A frown. A smile.

She's way more interesting than the movie. I could watch

her all night, the sparkle in her eyes, the softness of that lower lip.

And then she catches me in the act. She grabs the remote and hits pause.

"What?" she demands.

"You're just . . ." I'm not good with words. I've never been good with words. "I'm sorry."

But she doesn't hit play again. She just sits there, holding the remote, looking at me like I'm a puzzle she's trying to solve.

"Jack," she says finally. "Why did you stop talking to me? After you kissed me in the basement?"

I was so not expecting that. We've never talked about it. And I had no idea that if she brought it up, I would feel like this, like I'm walking on a tightrope.

"That was fourteen years ago."

"I know, but I've always wanted to know."

"I just—I was thirteen. Who knows why thirteen-year-old guys do anything? Why not ask me why I kissed you in the first place?"

"Why did you kiss me in the first place?"

Oh, Jesus, I'm an idiot. "Maddie."

She pins me with her gaze.

"Because I was a teenager and you were a girl and we were in an enclosed space," I lie. Or, well, not lie precisely, but conveniently simplify.

She looks disappointed. And honestly, I'm kind of disappointed in myself. Here we are, watching a movie where people keep lying about stuff, and I'm doing it too. So I take a deep breath and man up.

"I liked you." My voice sounds defensive, even to me. "I

kissed you because I liked you. I wanted to show you how much."

I've become a student of her expressions, watching her while she watches the movie, but this one is new. So soft and open I want to look away, like she's too vulnerable and it hurts to see it.

"I liked you, too," she says, and even though it's one of those phrases that can mean anything or nothing, my gut knows she means it in the anything way. "So how come you didn't talk to me after—?"

"I was a thirteen-year-old boy," I say firmly. "I was embarrassed. And then—"

I stop, abruptly.

"Then your dad left." She supplies it quietly. Gently.

"Then my dad left."

"And?"

She's always been like this. Direct. Asking questions I don't want to answer, making me face things I don't want to think about.

And everything fell apart. And the last thing I wanted was for Maddie to tell me it wasn't my fault and it was all going to be okay when I knew it was and it wouldn't be.

"There was too much shit," I say, because that's the truth, too, the simple truth.

She nods.

Then she picks up the remote control and starts the movie again. And I'm like—*Wait!*

But I don't know what I still need to say, or how I'd say it, even if I knew exactly what it was.

We watch the rest of the movie and then she gets up from

the couch and says, "Good night, Jack. That was really fun. Thanks for suggesting it."

And I say, "It *was* fun. Thanks for hanging out with me."

One last note on *Bend It Like Beckham.* I don't remember this movie being this stressful to watch the last time I saw it, which was admittedly a million years ago.

I don't remember it being so hard to watch two people who obviously care so much about each other have such a hard time showing it.

17

MADDIE

Saturday is my long day at work, and by the time I get home, Gabe is asleep in his bed and Jack is asleep on the couch in front of the television. I turn off the TV and the overhead light and throw a blanket over Jack. Asleep, his face is peaceful, his lashes absurdly long. He looks so much like Gabe that it makes my chest ache.

Maybe it's impossible not to have feelings for the man who contributed half the genes in your perfect child? Maybe the fact that I can't get Jack out of my blood is as much about gratitude for Gabe as anything else?

Without thinking about it, I press a quick kiss to Jack's forehead, the way I do when I come in at night to check on Gabe.

I feel the electric thrum he gives off before my lips even touch his skin. And then there's the smell of his skin and the ghost of his aftershave, both scents hard-wired directly between my legs. I practically jump back.

Yeah. The way Jack makes me feel? *Definitely* not only about his genetic contribution to my beautiful son.

I hurry down the hall, resisting the urge to look around guiltily, as if someone might have seen either the kiss or the chemical reaction it set off. I shed my work clothes, climb into bed, and crash like a ton of bricks. I don't even remember turning off the light.

I wake to a rare, violent spring thunderstorm.

Here's the thing. When I said that thunderstorms *freaked* me out, I meant thunderstorms *freak* me out. Like, still.

I know, I know. It's totally juvenile. You're supposed to get over thunderstorms when you get over volcanoes and tsunamis, but instead they ended up filed under Spiders and Snakes. Permanently stuck in my head as grounds for panic.

It's not rational. I don't actually think thunder is going to strike Jack's house and sizzle through his electrical system and burn out our brains.

Still, even at age twenty-six, every time there's a close clap of thunder, especially if it's almost right on the top of the lightning, as it is right now, I go into this hard-core adrenaline overload and get frozen and shaky.

The one thing stronger than my shock and terror is my worry for my kid, so I drag myself out of bed and creep down the hall to check on Gabe. He's sleeping straight through the racket, sacked out with his limbs flailed. I retrieve his covers from where he's flung them and tuck him in, and he barely stirs. I kiss his cheek and turn to head back down the hall.

Two things happen in rapid succession. Lightning flashes, illuminating a ghostly human figure in the hallway, and then, almost immediately, there is a clap of thunder.

The figure rushes toward me.

I scream, but since my throat has closed up, it's more like a squeak.

"For fuck's sake, Maddie!" says the ghost, "you haven't learned anything in sixteen years, have you?"

It's Jack, of course, and his arms are around me. I'm panting and clutching him and he's laughing—*laughing*—at me.

"It's not funny!" I cry.

But his laughter is contagious and his arms are tight and warm, and then I'm laughing too, the two of us hugging and shaking with hilarity. He sleeps in just those stupid pajama pants, so the bare skin of my arms is flush with the hot skin of his bare torso, and *wow*, the heat and charge pouring off him could set me on fire.

Suddenly neither of us is laughing. We cling to each other and his breath is as fast and shallow as mine. He adjusts his position to bring the whole length of my body in line with his.

He feels so good. So warm, so fiercely alive, so strong and safe.

And then his head dips and his mouth finds mine.

"Oh, fuck," he says, almost immediately, by which I think he means *Oh my God this is good,* but there's no time to ask him because he's kissing me again, like I'm the best thing he's ever tasted and like he's never going to let me go, and I'm drowning in how good he tastes and feels.

He pulls away. "We can't do this here."

I clutch both his arms to prevent him from pulling away, which makes him laugh again.

"I didn't say we can't do this. I just said we can't do it here." He scoops me up and carries me down the hall, depositing me in my bed. I don't know if it's the terror or the relief or the fact that it's the middle of the night and it might be a dream, but I let it happen. He fastens the latch on the door, and for a split second I hate what that latch implies about Jack's extracurriculars, but then I don't care at all. I'm just grateful it's there.

He strides back to the bed. He hesitates, then, and I'm afraid he's going to stop us, now that I've decided I don't want him to, but he just says, "What the hell are we going to do with you, Maddie Adams?"

It's a rhetorical question, because he seems to know exactly what he wants to do with me. He climbs over me, one knee on each side, lowers himself to his elbows, and begins kissing me again, his mouth softer now, exploring, teasing, stroking. Each touch echoes in other parts of my body, lighten me up all over.

The hum of his moan vibrates through my lips and my tongue, through all my nerves, and his weight settles between my legs, the length of him there, the thickness and hardness, and I can feel that he's holding himself in check, wanting to move against me, but neither of us wants this to end too fast. So I hold still, too, under him, even though my body is aching, calling out to his. Instead, I touch him with my fingertips everywhere I can reach, all that bareness mine, the groove of his spine, the curve of his ass under the pajama pants, my hands so greedy for the heat and silk of him.

He's worked both hands under my T-shirt, and when he finds my breasts bare, he makes a noise halfway between a grunt and a groan and catches my nipples in his fingers, then pushes the T-shirt up over my head and buries his face in my breasts. The roughness of his stubble and the hot, wet softness of his mouth wreck me. I'm all sensation, lost to the pinch and flick and swirl of his teeth and tongue. I don't even realize that I'm tipping my hips to get more of him until he puts a hand on my hip bone and gently pushes down, scolding, "Be patient."

"Can't. Jack—"

He kisses me again and I'm moaning into his mouth, trying to thrust against him. One of his hands finds the waistband of my sweatpants and works them down between us, so it's just my teeny-tiny panties, those flimsy pajamas pants, and the magic of Jack. I slide a hand under the elastic of his pants and find him. The heft, the solidity, the rare wonder of chamois-soft skin over steel, sends more slick heat to my core. "Mmmm, Jack. You're big."

"I've been told," he says, the words a groan.

I swirl a thumb through the slickness he's shed for me, around the sensitive head, and he bucks. He grabs my wrist in his big hand. "Stop that."

"I want to touch you."

"Well, I want to fuck you and I'm not going to last long enough if you keep that up. What do you think of that?" he murmurs against my ear, his breath spreading tingles everywhere.

A few hours ago I was sure I wasn't going to let anything like this happen. A few minutes ago I was planning to call a halt at naked groping.

Now there is no doubt at all in my mind what I want.

"I want you to."

"You want me to what?" he demands.

I shake my head.

"Say it."

"I want you to fuck me," I whisper.

"Again."

His voice is rough, a groan, and it sends a sharp, hot thrill through me. "I want you to fuck me."

"Tell me I'm big again."

That makes me groan. "You are. You're big, and you're going to feel really good inside me—"

"Oh my God, Maddie—"

"So you should probably go get a condom right now."

He has that glazed, lost look that tells me he's in no shape for higher reasoning, so I instruct him: "There's a box in my bottom dresser drawer."

He stumbles in his haste, which makes me laugh, and then, once he's retrieved the prize, he stands at the side of the bed and tears the packet open.

"Gimme." I hold my hand out.

I roll it on while he watches, his eyes narrowed to slits, teeth gritted. He throbs under my touch.

Then I reach up and he tumbles back into my arms, kissing and kissing me, slick, dark, fine. I don't know how long we kiss for, skin sliding against skin, because I'm lost in my own hunger, in his rough breathing, in the press of his thigh between mine.

He slides a hand down my belly and slips his fingers between my legs, where he finds me swollen and eager.

"Mmm," he says, playing a little. Trailing his fingers through the wet heat there, teasing my clit with the slightest touch, while I try to tip my hips up to get more contact, more sensation.

"Jack."

"Yeah."

"Please."

That makes him grin.

"Please what?"

"Please fuck me."

He braces himself up on those amazing sculpted arms, his chest filling my visual field with that absurd golden male beauty of his, and I guide him to me.

He stops there.

"Don't tease."

"I'm. Not. Teasing," he says with difficulty. "I'm trying not to embarrass myself."

And then he eases into me, just the head. The sensation of being penetrated by him makes me gasp, it's so good, the pressure and the heat and the sheer, unbeatable thickness.

I whimper. "Now you're teasing."

He grins. "Now I'm teasing."

It is so, so hard to hold still under him. I hope it's as difficult for him as it is for me. I look at where we're joined, then up at his face. His jaw is set in concentration.

"It's just, I fucking love this part, you know?" he says reverently. "Where you're resisting me and I'm asking you to let me in, and you're so tight but opening to me, and getting wetter, and I can watch the whole thing on your face. First *yes, please,* and then, *more, please,* and then, *come on, Jack, give it to me.* Your face . . ."

There is something about the way he says *your face* that makes me know he means *me.* Not just a generic woman's face, but mine.

"You show it all to me. You give it all to me. You love it, and that makes me love it. I want to do this part all day. You know?"

I nod, helpless. He eases forward another, I don't know, millimeter, and my whole body is crying out for him. Like I'm this huge, empty space and he is the everything that's going to rush in and make it okay. And I know that's just the way it's supposed to work; that's the way sex works, right? I'm the empty vessel, he's the thing that fills me, I'm supposed to feel this mad craving for him, but just like when he said *your face* he meant mine, when I say I want to be filled, I mean *by him.*

He takes it so slow that I feel like I'm melting around him. Like I'm this pool of molten gold and he's the furnace, and instead of pushing against resistance now he's just stirring and stoking the heat of me, and the orgasm begins as just this whisper of desperation and builds and builds and builds until when he finally gives me the final inch of himself and then the last fraction behind that, I don't so much break or shatter as flow out from myself in swirl after swirl after swirl, crying his name as quietly as I can.

18

______

JACK

"**I** lied," I say.

Maddie opens her eyes. "Whaa?"

She is pretty wrecked, which makes me exceptionally happy. That orgasm looked—well, it looked like it felt terrific, obviously, but also kind of like she was listening to a broadcast from outer space, you know? Like, she was so far away from me, so far inside her pleasure, that it almost hurt to see.

Now she's back, watching me with a hazy look on her relaxed face. I am still buried to the hilt in her, and she is clenching around me, aftershocks, and every one of those spasms threatens to push me over the edge. I have to concentrate with all my mental capacity to keep from coming.

"*This* is my favorite part," I say. "When you're all satisfied and just lying there lazily watching me and you're all swollen up and tight and every time I thrust—"

I illustrate, and she makes a noise that sounds almost like pain, except I know it's not.

"—you make that little noise."

Because I remember. I remember all these things about Maddie from before.

I do it again, a few more times, for good measure, and her head falls back against the pillow and her face flushes and I'm pretty sure I'm going to be able to make her come again, and easily.

If I hadn't been teetering on the edge before, I am now. Each thrust feels so damn good, from the tip of my cock to the base and deep in my balls, not to mention that place low in my gut, almost at the bottom of my spine, where it's all gathering itself for an epic orgasm.

"C'mon, baby," I cajole, and her eyes go a notch darker and she makes that noise—whimper, moan, I don't know what you call it, Maddie's sex noise. I thrust myself deep into her, feeling the heat and squeeze and hug of her around me, the long, sweet strokes of pleasure with no real beginning and no real end, and when I'm as deep as I can go and just a little deeper, I circle my hips and her eyes roll back in her head and she starts making her signature sounds one right after the other, whimper-grunts of satisfaction and need.

"I love watching you," I tell her, and her pupils shrink and her blush gets deeper. She looks right back at me, her gaze locked onto mine.

I might be sorry later that I've said all this. But I'm not sorry now. It needs to be said. She needs to know. When someone makes you feel this good, you have to give her full credit and thank her for it however you can. Right now I'm thanking her by relentlessly continuing the bump and grind of my pelvis against hers. And I'm watching need rise in her face as color, like sap in a tree in the spring, and I watch and watch until I lose track of holding myself back and she's coming again and I'm coming, every muscle in my body rigid and shaking, pleasure roaring up my spine and swamping me.

I collapse half on top of her, half next to her, trying not to crush her.

"Fuck, Jack," she says. "That was . . ."

We both laugh because she's clearly not going to finish the sentence.

"There are no words?"

"There are no words."

And then we're both quiet for a minute. I think we're both remembering.

AFTER I FUCKED twenty-one-year-old Maddie against the wall of the boathouse in the woods near Revere Lake, I helped her unwind her legs from around me and set her back on the floor. She wobbled a little, and I reached out to steady her.

I'd had a lot of sex by that point in my life. Drunk, sober, stoned, in bed, against walls, on horizontal non-bed surfaces, with high school girls starting when I was fourteen, and later women, older women and younger women, women who wanted to stay over afterward and women who were as happy as I was to scratch an itch and move on.

Before Maddie, I used to say there was no such thing as "bad sex." All sex was at least "good." Some sex was "very good" or "fucking awesome." Some women could do stuff with their mouths or their hands or their pussies that should be celebrated in a Sexual Hall of Fame. Some could energetically bounce themselves on a dick in ways that defied gravity.

The sex that Maddie and I had just had was a different beast entirely. It wasn't a physical act. It didn't seem to be about sexual skill or experience at all, although something superhuman had definitely helped me take her up against that wall. It was about how it felt to see Maddie crying on the shore of the lake. How it felt to take Maddie in my arms and discover that she was perfectly familiar, like I'd held her a thousand times already. How it felt to kiss her like we could just pick up where we'd left off when I was thirteen.

How it felt to bury myself inside her and forget everything else.

My chest tightened. I'd just started to come down off the sex high and remembered that she was going to go back to college. And even if she weren't going back to college, she was Maddie Adams and I was Jack Parker and this sex wasn't a thing that could keep happening. It was a moment in time, like a shooting star.

"Jack," Maddie said. Her voice was unsteady. "Are you always that good?"

I laughed. I couldn't help it. And I wanted to tell her what I'd just realized: that no one is that good by himself, that it always takes two, but—

It was too fucking complicated and she was leaving.

"Yup," I said.

I was that kind of asshole.

She sighed.

I helped her put herself back together. She smoothed her hair down and wiped a finger under each of her eyes to get rid of the smeared mascara.

"Okay?" she asked, showing me her handiwork.

She was so pretty, even with lake-damp hair and messed-up makeup. Maybe more so because I'd been the one to ruin the makeup. "You look—" I'd been about to say "beautiful," but I didn't want to sound like a tool. I'd just fucked a good girl against the rough wood wall of a boathouse with the smell of mildew all around us, and now I was going to send her back into the world with my cum still hot between her legs, and telling her she was beautiful would be a sad half-assed attempt to make us both feel like we hadn't crossed some line that shouldn't be crossed.

"You look fine," I said roughly.

I thought that was it. I hugged her and she walked away, and five minutes later I walked out of the boathouse, and I don't think anyone gave our disappearances and reappearances a second thought. Maybe Maddie told Mia what we'd done, and maybe she didn't; maybe she was starting to feel shame about fucking in a boathouse or against a wall or with all her clothes on or for one-night-only, or because it was me and I wasn't the kind of guy she'd seriously date. But overall, I felt like we could both pretend it hadn't happened. And that was good.

Right?

Wrong.

I couldn't sleep. I couldn't sleep that night, and I couldn't sleep the night after, and nothing I did—not mining the spank bank for every kinky hookup I'd ever had, not counting sheep, not going for a 1 a.m. run—nothing helped.

I just wanted her. It was so plain and simple and elemental. I wanted her. Up against the wall of a boathouse. In the sand, at the water's edge. In my truck, over my kitchen table, in my bed.

But I might have resisted. I might have.

She was the one who showed up at my apartment, three nights after the party at the lake. I was in a studio over the drugstore at that point, and she rang the doorbell. I opened the door and there she was, wearing a flimsy sundress and looking uncertain.

"What are you doing here?" I asked, confirming my asshole status.

"I don't know."

It was so honest, and she looked so lost, that I opened the door wide and let her in. I let her sit down on my couch, and I poured her a beer and we sat awkwardly.

"No," she said suddenly. "That's a lie. I know why I'm here."

I raised an eyebrow.

"I want to do it again."

"You. Want. To—?" Pretty sure my mouth was hanging open.

"I want to have sex with you again."

"You know that's not how it usually works. You don't just show up and tell someone—"

"Fine," she said, crossing her arms. "Tell me you want me to go. Tell me you don't want to have sex with me. I'll leave, I'll leave you alone, and that will be it."

She glared at me, all dare and challenge.

I thought about it. About telling her I didn't want to have sex. About her walking out the door. About me closing the door behind her and spending tonight the way I'd spent the last two nights, with my hand on my dick and my mind hopelessly tangled up in the way sex with Maddie had made me feel.

Then I thought about telling her the truth. That I hadn't

stopped thinking about what we'd done for five minutes straight. That I was hard as a rock, that I'd been hard more or less as soon as I'd seen her in that sundress, that when she'd said she wanted to do it again I'd nearly passed out from the rush of blood from my head to what I'd thought was an already fully flushed dick.

The first way was smarter. Safer. Neater. But I couldn't make myself take it.

"I lied, too," I said, my heart galloping.

It was her turn to raise an eyebrow.

"When you asked, after we fucked, if I was always that good? The answer is no. I've never been that good. It wasn't me."

"If it wasn't you, who was it?" She looked hopelessly confused.

"I mean, it wasn't just me. It was us. How we were together. We were that good."

She made a soft, surprised noise. Pleased. She licked her lips.

I wanted my tongue where hers had just been.

"Come here," I said.

She did.

We had sex fifteen more times during nine more nights over a total of seventeen days.

I don't seem like the kind of guy who would remember those numbers, do I?

I remember *everything*.

19

———

MADDIE

Jack gets up to throw away the condom. And I wait in the bed, unsure about what will happen next. Or what I want to happen next.

He comes back and slides under the covers beside me. I roll close to him, rest my head on his chest. He puts his arms around me and kisses my hair.

I'm flooded with warmth and relief. Also sadness. Because he just made me feel so good, so happy. And it's so —temporary.

"Maddie," he whispers.

"Mmm-hmm."

"I want to do it again."

I smile against the groove where chest meets shoulder. "Right now?"

"Fifteen minutes from now," he says decisively. "And possibly one or two more times before the sun comes up. And tomorrow night. Can we do it again tomorrow night?"

I laugh. But part of me isn't laughing. The part that's watching from a little outside the situation, thinking, *How do*

I protect myself from this? From the way he makes me feel and the way he makes me laugh?

"Jack," I whisper.

"Mmm-hmm."

"Just while I'm living here, right? When I move out, it's a logical end point, and then we don't have to do the awkward dance when one of us is ready to move on. I don't want this to make things complicated between us, because we still have to do what's right for Gabe. I mean, I'm on the rebound, and you're—you've been honest from the beginning about liking your life the way it is."

I want him to contradict me. I want him to say, *That was then; this is now. I'm ready to have my life be different. I'm ready to have my life include you and Gabe.*

He's quiet. Then he says, "That's smart. Yeah. Just while you're living here."

I'm still lying in the same spot, my cheek against his skin. His arms are still around me. But I feel a chill I can't shake.

He shifts suddenly under me, and for a moment I think he's pulling away. Then I realize he's sliding down under the covers, turning as he goes, his mouth trailing across my collarbone and finding a nipple. His hand settles over my other breast, and the contrast between what he's doing with his mouth—the barest, slightest flitters of sensation, toying with me with his tongue—and what he's doing with his hand —rolling my nipple tight between two skilled fingers—has me gasping in a second.

"Jack—"

"I like the sound of that," he murmurs against my breast. He backs off my nipple and teases me with light fingertips, circling closer and closer to where I'm drawn tight but not quite touching it, until, the next time I say his name, I'm pleading.

Then he slowly trails his mouth down my belly, until his shoulders are pushing my legs apart. He pauses there, blowing lightly across my curls, using those callused fingertips to trickle sensation across my spread thighs, touching his lips down here and there until he has me squirming.

He uses his thumbs to open me.

"You're so pretty," he says, slicking my moisture all over me, teasing the folds and curves, finding my clit with one fingertip. Then his mouth replaces his fingers, and the whole world shrinks to what he's doing, to the warm flat and skillful tip of his tongue, to broad strokes and swirls and flicks and the gathering, tightening, urgent, God, *violent* need he's conjuring out of me, and then I'm coming, coming, coming, coming.

When I open my eyes, I find him grinning at me over my pubic bone.

"Well," he says dryly. "Look at us making the most of the shitty housing market."

20

MADDIE

I'm on my way home from work the next night, Sunday, when I get a phone call from a landlord I'd called a few days earlier about an apartment. It's a two-bedroom in Ballard, and it had sounded really promising from the description.

As per Jack's wishes, we had (amazing) sex again twice more last night after he went down on me. "We're going to do this as much we possibly can until our time runs out," he said, after his third and my sixth orgasm, right before I sent him back to his room. Light was beginning to seep in the window and Gabe would be up soon.

It was a brutal day of work on just a couple of hours' sleep, but orgasms have magical power to combat sleep deprivation, so I managed to be pretty cheerful through all the usual workday crises. So much so that one of my coworkers asked me if I had any good news to share with her.

Somehow, *I'm doing the dirty (again) with my baby daddy* wasn't going to come out sounding like something I should be celebrating, so I kept my mouth shut about that and just shrugged and said I was in a good mood.

When the call about the apartment comes through, I almost tell the landlord I'm not interested in seeing the place anymore. It's pretty hard, after what happened last night, to imagine just blithely continuing the apartment hunt. And yet, what else can I do? I can't squat at Jack's house forever, and both of us know sex between us has to have a definite end. Because: history and hurt and incompatible views of monogamy and family.

So I head into Ballard to take a look at the apartment. And I'm glad I did. It's small but beautiful—two tiny bedrooms, and a combo living room–kitchen with huge windows. Wood floors, in reasonably decent condition, and a bathroom that looks like it was redone in the last couple of years.

Of course, I'm flooded with mixed feelings. So much relief at finding a place that's perfect for Gabe and me. But also fear that we won't get it. The landlord told me, just before she took me through, that she had already shown it to a couple of people earlier today. I couldn't get here any sooner, though, because of work.

On top of all that, there's my ambivalence about leaving Jack's place. Because it's one thing to put an expiration date on the sex and something else entirely to know that it's just ten days out. This place is available in a week and a half.

But the truth is, I really need this apartment to be The One. I need a decent, safe place for Gabe and me to live, and I need to get out of Jack's house before I get in any deeper than I already am. Which is starting to seem more and more likely. Not just because of the sex, but because of moments like the one Friday night when we were watching the movie together. Those moments aren't about chemistry or the size of Jack's package or how well he knows my body. They're about Jack and me and how easy it is to be with him, like it always has been. And that's the problem.

I could fall right back into it. I could fall right back in love with him.

So as tempting as it is to postpone the inevitable, as tempting as it is to, as Jack put it, reap some benefits from the shitty housing market, I need to get this apartment and get out of Jack's house. I need to have my eyes fixed on that prize.

I come out of the bathroom to find the landlord on the phone, and I can tell from the look she gives me, even before I hear her say, "You can email the application to—" that I'm not going to get the apartment.

She hangs up and says, "The woman I showed it to right before you is sending me an application."

"So I'm too late?"

She's sixtyish, with big green-framed glasses and gray hair that looks like it's been set over her head like a helmet. She tilts her head and examines me thoughtfully. "I'll take your application if you can get it to me tonight. Email it to me." She hands me a card. "But," she says sternly. I think she is probably a schoolteacher or someone else used to keeping troublemakers in line. "Unless there's something missing from her application or she doesn't qualify, Seattle law says I have to let her have it. She was here first."

I know the law she's talking about. It was put in place to combat racism and other forms of discrimination in the housing process. I appreciate the fact that she knows the law and wants to follow it. So even though part of me is still tempted to beg her for the apartment, I give her my email address so she can send me the application, and then I follow her out of the building and trudge back to my car.

In the car, I pull my laptop out of my backpack, find the landlord's email, fill out the application, and hit send. I'm not going to leave anything to chance that I can control. And I'm not even going to let myself feel hopeful about this place. I filled out the application, sure, but I'm going to assume it's a lost cause. That way I can't be too disappointed when I don't get it.

Or too relieved, I think, before I can stop myself.

I sigh.

As much as I want to find a place to stay, I'm dead on my feet after a week of working and apartment hunting, and there's nothing promising left on my list of prospects.

I guess I'm heading back to Jack's house.

As I get close, my heart beats a little faster, my adrenaline rising. I tell myself that the eagerness I feel to get home is about wanting to see Gabe and nothing else. Not about Jack.

When I pull up in front of Jack's house, his mom's and Sienna's cars are in the driveway. And even though I figured they'd probably be there—Jack had said they were going to come spend the afternoon and evening with Gabe—I'm instantly bummed. I don't feel like talking about the failed apartment hunt with a bunch of people who don't necessarily have my back. I want—

I want to go back to bed with Jack. But that's maybe not the best idea ever. Every time he makes me feel the way he did last night, I'm going to slide closer to feeling like I want sex with Jack to be a permanent fixture in my life. Closer to feeling like I want *Jack* to be a permanent fixture in my life.

So maybe it's a blessing that Jack's mother and sister are here tonight. They'll make a great buffer.

They're sitting in the living room. Sienna and Jack have beers in front of them, Linda has a glass of wine, and they're playing Hearts.

"Hey," Sienna says, smiling at me as I shut the door behind me. "Give me a minute. I'm about to win."

"Hello, Maddie," Linda says formally—no smile.

"Hi," I say, feeling shy.

As I watch, Sienna's prediction comes true. Linda's total tops a hundred, ending the game, and Sienna has the lowest score.

"Can we deal you in?" Sienna tilts her head.

I start to wave my hand (*so exhausted, heading off to bed*), but Jack looks up and gives me a lopsided smile that I can feel in about a hundred separate places, and I find myself plopping onto the sofa beside him.

"How was the house-hunting?" he asks, as Sienna deals.

"I found this amazing place—" I begin.

"Oh, good," Linda says. "I was just saying to Jack, you two need to be out of each other's hair."

I'm already regretting having sat down. Linda has never tried to hide her feelings toward me. I guess it's not too shocking: I'm the woman who trapped her baby boy.

"Mom, Jack's already told you that's not true." Sienna turns to me. "He said it's been nothing but great having you guys here," she tells me warmly, and then mouths, *Sorry,* rolling her eyes toward her mother.

I'm more surprised by Sienna's coming to my rescue than by Linda's attack. Like I said, I pretty much know where I stand with Linda. But I've never been so sure with Sienna.

When we were little, Sienna sometimes played with Jack and me, but more often, she was off with girls her age, and I was already a senior when Sienna started high school, so I never knew her well. Whenever we've crossed paths since then—those occasional holiday dinners, drop-offs and pickups—she's always been kind, but I've always felt like there was a distance between us. At first I thought it might be judgment. But she's never said anything to make me feel like she holds the accidental pregnancy, or Jack's decision to support Gabe financially, against me. And she obviously loves Gabe like crazy, would do anything for him.

I shoot her a grateful smile, and she smiles back.

"So you found a place?" Jack asks. I can't read the expression on his face.

"I did, but I'm probably not going to get it. The landlord had already taken one application, and she said that unless something was wrong with that one, I'd be second in line."

His mother gives a sigh of obvious disappointment.

"That sucks," Jack says.

It does, of course it does, but some stupid, juvenile part of me wishes he'd said something else. Like, *Good. I'm not ready to let you and Gabe go yet.*

Fat fucking chance, I chastise myself.

"Fingers crossed," Sienna says.

"I'm trying not to get my hopes up."

I sneak a look at Jack, and he looks back. And there's a moment, just a moment, where I think we might be on the same page. Like, *I don't know what to want anymore. Not sure which way my hopes are even headed.* I get a giddy swirl in my chest, and then—

Fear, of course. Like a lead blanket on the giddy.

"Everyone in?" Sienna asks, and when we all nod, she deals.

It's been a long time since I've played Hearts, and the rest of them are all warmed up, so it's clear I'm getting my butt kicked. Meanwhile, I do my best to try to draw Linda into conversation, asking about her trip, asking how things are going with her librarian job—but it's like squeezing water from a stone.

"Mom. Tell Maddie about the game you were playing with Gabe," Sienna says.

"It was just a game," Linda says, playing into the current trick, then taking it.

Sienna rolls her eyes at me again, and the unexpected solidarity, especially in light of the family relationships, makes me feel teary. I guess when you're feeling suddenly short on girlfriends, it doesn't take much.

Sienna and I could be friends, I think.

The eager little jump in my stomach is followed by me getting a firm grip on myself:

I. Don't. Live. Here.

This isn't my life, and I have to remember that.

Jack takes the next trick and winks at me. Oh, God, the wink. He taught himself how to wink when he was ten. Even then, before it should have had any power over me, it made me feel off balance.

"She put all the couch cushions on the floor and they took off their shoes—" Sienna begins.

Linda cannot resist. "The rules are," she says primly, scooping up the next set of cards, "you can't step on the carpet. Only the cushions. The carpet is molten lava."

"Oh, God, he must have loved that." I can picture Gabe

hooting with joy as he tiptoed and jumped from cushion to cushion. It's exactly up his alley.

"Oh, he did," Linda says, growing more animated. "He was hopping around, saying, 'Gramma, you be careful! You be careful!' You should have seen him. And when he 'fell in,' I had to fish him out, and I made it very dramatic—"

She stops as if she's suddenly realized she's sharing a moment with the enemy. Then smiles at me almost shyly.

"He's a good kid," she says. She sounds reluctant, but —kind.

My stomach warms.

Then lurches.

I. Don't.

Live. Here.

Linda wins.

She crows wildly, lording it over all of us. But I don't mind at all, because she includes me in the lording, and she's clearly having a good time. And I think about the Linda I knew as a girl, tight-lipped, with bruised dark skin under her eyes.

This Linda looks . . . she looks relaxed. Free.

And Sienna, too—Sienna was one of those girls who was always a little wary. Like she was braced for something to go wrong. But now she's laughing at her mother's antics and casting friendly glances my way. She seems like she's grown into young adulthood beautifully.

I guess maybe Jack's dad leaving was the best thing that

could have happened to either of those women, in the long run.

If only Jack could be like that, too. If he could see his father's leaving as a blessing, instead of more evidence that he wasn't worth loving.

Linda and Sienna get to their feet, carry their glasses into the kitchen, and help clean up the snacks and the cards. "Hey," Sienna says. "Some friends and I are going to see *Romy and Michele's High School Reunion,* the musical version, at the Fifth Avenue Theater Tuesday night. I have a couple of extra tickets. Any interest?"

I think my mouth falls open.

My immediate response is *Yes!* Like the kind of yes where if she were actually holding the tickets in her hand, I would have to sit on my hands to keep from grabbing at them.

The yes isn't for the particular musical, which I don't know anything about, or the theater—it's for how much I'd like to be Sienna's friend.

But—

I don't live here. This isn't my life.

She must sense my hesitation. "I know you might have found a new place by then, but then it'll be even easier, right? If you're in the city?"

"I'll have to find someone to watch Gabe."

"I can," Jack and Linda say at the same time.

Do you know that thing they say about how when God shuts a door, he opens a window? Standing in Harris's apartment, looking at the wreckage of my life, I felt so wretched.

And now I feel lucky. I have things to do, places to go, people to hang with, and family to help me. Even if the luck terrifies me a little (because it can't hold, can it?), I am not stupid enough to cast it off.

"Sure," I say.

Sienna grins, pleased, which makes me grin too, until we're grinning at each other like crazy fools. She and Linda hug Jack good night, and then they hug me—Linda is a warm, soft, grandmotherly cloud of Tide laundry soap, Sienna a sharp, bony hugger who still manages to convey affection in the tightness of her grip. They head out into the night and I'm left standing in the living room while Jack shuts the door and turns toward me.

21

———

JACK

"So," I say. "You might have an apartment."

I'm happy for her. Of course I'm happy for her. She took a body blow with that bullshit from Harris and Mia, and she needs to get back on her feet.

She nods.

She looks so beautiful right now. Her hair's down around her face, soft and sleek, and she's got a bright glow under her skin.

I take alpha male pride in having put that glow on her. And yeah, thinking about exactly how I put that glow on her makes me ready to do it again. Like right now.

She was so fucking hot last night. Moaning into my mouth, talking dirty, tight as a glove around me, coming so sweetly. Later, having my mouth on her again—no one tastes or feels like Maddie. And then twice more before morning, each time hotter than the last.

"Finding an apartment is good, right?"

I want her to argue with me, to say, *Hell no, not with sex like last night's on the table.*

"Yeah, it's good."

Of course it's fucking good. So why does it feel so bad? It's not like I thought what happened last night could go on forever. Been there, done that, blown it hard. Given enough time, I would screw it up again.

Better not to give it that much time. Hurts so much less.

Maddie shakes her head. "I probably won't get it. I'm telling myself I won't, so I won't be disappointed when I inevitably lose it."

She's saying she'll be disappointed if she loses the apartment. What, disappointed if she has to stay with me and keep having sex like we had last night? If she has to come so hard her toes cramp?

I put that in my pipe and smoke it, feeling—irritable. "Because it's hell staying here."

She looks at me, eyes big and startled. "No! No, that's not what I meant. You've been—great. It's just—I mean, what your mom said. We should get out of each other's hair. You can have your social life back—"

She says *social life* in this way that makes it obvious what she means—*sex with lots and lots of women*—and I'm pissed. Because she's okay with that, right? She's okay with—even advocating for—the possibility of me being able to bring women back here and fuck them, when I can't imagine being okay with the idea of her having sex with anyone other than me ever again—

Screeeeeeech.

Those are the brakes in my head.

She's shaking her head. "I'm probably not going to get the apartment. And I'm kind of freaked out about that. I mean, I've spent, what, like, twenty hours looking at apartments, and there's nothing I can bring Gabe into, and when I finally find something that's halfway decent, someone's beaten me to it."

I wrench my head out of my ass and focus on what's right in front of me, which is Maddie, looking like she's going to cry again.

I wish she wouldn't.

I hope she does, because if she does, I will have the excuse I desperately want to put my arms around her and—

And everything. Fucking everything. Bite that amazing, plump lower lip, slide my tongue along hers until she whimpers, eat her mouth until all she can think about is me doing the same thing to her pussy.

"I'm basically homeless right now, Jack—"

Annnnd, once again, I'm an asshole.

I need to be happy for her about this apartment. Because it's what she wants and needs, because it's what Gabe needs, and because it's probably what I need, too. I'm just being selfish, wanting to keep her here for my own deranged, horny purposes, when she could be finding another guy—

Okay, screw that.

Just because I'm not enough of a jerk to outright interfere with her happiness doesn't mean I'm in a hurry to give up sex with Maddie. And it sure as hell doesn't mean I want to think about her finding herself a new Big Dick.

"You're not homeless. You can stay here as long as you need to," I say. Selfish, maybe, but it's also true.

She gets that look on her face again. The soft, wrecked one. And now I'm the one who feels like crying. So I do what I always do when things get too real. I make a joke. "You don't even have to have sex with me if you don't want to."

The corners of her mouth turn up. Now she looks like mischief. She tilts her head. "So, you're saying that if I said I was really tired right now and just wanted to go straight to bed . . ."

"Not a problem." I wave my hand generously.

". . . instead of dragging you into my room and kneeling at your feet and giving you the best head of your life . . ."

It is very, very hard to get the best of Maddie in any kind of verbal play situation.

It is also just very, very hard. Or getting there, anyway.

Two can play, though, right? "I'd be fine with that."

She narrows her eyes.

"I'm a big boy," I say. "I can take care of myself."

To illustrate, I slide the flat of my hand over the growing bulge behind the fly of my jeans. It is getting pretty uncomfortable in there, but she doesn't need to know that. She also doesn't need to know that I'd take the warmth of her mouth over my own fist in a heartbeat.

Her gaze follows my hand, her eyes dark and avid, but to give her credit, she manages to look pretty nonchalant. "Okay, then." She shrugs. "Good night, I guess." And she strolls out of my living room toward her room.

I wait for her to turn back, laughing, but she doesn't. She goes into her room, pulling the door shut behind her. I race after her and wedge my foot in with just a second to spare.

"Why, Jack!" she says, with mock surprise. "What are you doing here?"

"Collecting rent," I growl, pushing my way into her room and closing the door behind me.

She giggles.

"Seriously, Maddie, you can't just say shit like that—"

She gives me a super-wide-eyed innocent look. "But Jack, you said you'd be fine on your own!"

"I will," I say, undoing the top button of my jeans. "You just watch." And I undo the next few buttons—which is not easy to do, because my dick is so hard behind my fly that I have trouble getting my fingers under the buttons.

Her eyes are glued to the proceedings.

"See?" I ask. "Totally capable of managing this situation." I push my briefs down, freeing my dick.

Her pupils flare, and her tongue peeks out to wet her lips. My plans call for that tongue to do a lot more than play peek-aboo in the next few minutes, but there's plenty of time for that. I stroke my hand idly down my length, smoothing a drop of pre-cum over the head as I go. I don't have to fake my groan, which is half from how good it feels to be this hard and half from watching her eyes follow my hand.

"How many strokes do you think it will take me?" I ask her, all casual-like. I push my briefs and jeans a little lower so I can cup my balls and drag my hand back up the whole length. I make that single stroke take a good, long time, and then I play around the head a little while her mouth goes slack.

"One," I say, a quick, hard thrust into my hand.

It's not the tightness of my fist or the slickness of the pre-cum or the tease of the count that's killing me. It's the expression on her face. She looks like she's in pain, and it goes straight to my dick.

"Two."

She sways a little on her feet, leaning toward me.

"God, Maddie," I say. I have to stop with the strokes and squeeze the base. I was planning to tease her as long as it took, but I think I might be losing at my own game. As if to prove the point, my dick throbs, eking more pleasure out of the squeeze of my fist. It feels so good that for a moment I think I'm going to lose control, just like that, the two of us in this stupid standoff, me with my hand clenched around the base of my dick, not even moving. I can feel the heat high in my chest and face, and if she can't tell from that how close I am, I'm sure she can see how tight every muscle in my body is at my effort to stay in control of this encounter.

Then she drops to her knees at my feet and we both let out a simultaneous gust of breath. Her mouth caps my fist, surrounding the head of my dick with wet heat.

I swear colorfully. It's like she just turned the volume up to ten, and I'd thought it was already there.

Then she lets go, tips her head back, and smirks at me. "How's this for a game? I see how fast I can make you come, and you see how long you can hold out."

I squeeze against the rush of blood and pleasure, managing not to give myself away with any other sound or reaction. I've got this. I've totally got this.

Because I pride myself on this very thing. I will never come in a woman's mouth unless I know she wants me to. And blow jobs, although they're one of my favorite ways to pass a quiet evening, don't tend to make me come that easily. I don't know if it's that I need more depth, or more friction, or to be free from the threat of teeth, or just to be sure I'm not imposing myself on anyone (I'm big, as Maddie noted, and not every woman loves that; I've called off quite a few blow jobs midway through because the giver didn't look like she wanted that much of me in her face, and it's no fun to be an unwelcome presence).

So whatever, I figure I'm in my element now. Maddie'll suck and lick to her heart's content, and when she cries uncle, I'll win the game and finish us both missionary style.

She licks around the head a few times, curling her tongue in a way that makes it feel like she has two. Okay, so the girl has hops, I'll give her that. Then she flattens her tongue along the bottom of my dick, so when she moves up and down on me, there's a whole lot of extra heat and sensation, and suddenly I'm not at all sure I've got this.

Now she's doing both at the same time. How is that even possible? And I'm deep in her mouth, so deep I pull back a little because I'm worried about hurting her or choking her, but when I pull away she grabs my ass. And tugs me closer. My dick feels huge, flush with blood, flooded with sensation from root to tip, and the tide's rising at the bottom of my spine, in the depths of my gut—

"Maddie, I—"

But I'm coming so hard I can't stop it and I can't pull away from her and besides, she's got both hands on me now and I feel her swallow, like she's swallowing *me,* as I'm spurting into her mouth.

"I—didn't—mean—"

I have to put out a hand to brace myself against the wall, because my legs are about to collapse.

She lets me slide from between her swollen red lips and grins up at me. And laughs at my expression.

22

JACK

"Those smell like ass," Brooks tells Henry, who's eating hard-boiled eggs on the retaining wall. Brooks and Chase are both joining us for lunch today.

"Maybe like *your* ass," Henry says. "I wipe."

"Boys," I chastise, grade-school-teacher style.

It's Wednesday, a mile-high hump in the middle of another butt-ugly week at work. Except that my mind is a hundred miles away most of the time, in bed with Maddie, blown away by her skill and enthusiasm and the heat of her skin.

"Guess what I've got on my desk at home," Brooks says. He doesn't wait for us to guess, but crows, "March Madness championship tickets!"

Henry pumps a fist. "Phoenix, here we come!

In the silence that follows, all three of my friends turn to look at me. It's like facing a panel of judges.

"Don't even say it," Brooks warns.

"I don't know," I admit quietly.

"What do you mean, you don't know?" Henry demands.

"Maddie hasn't found a place to live yet."

"And that's your problem, how?"

"It's a really tough market. She's been looking and looking, but if she's still looking, she might need me to watch Gabe—"

Brooks makes a sound of the utmost disgust.

"Your mother can watch Gabe," Henry says. "Your sister can watch Gabe. This is March Madness. This is Phoenix. This is what matters in life. We may never get a chance like this again."

"It's complicated," I say, before I can think better of it.

Suddenly they are all staring at me again. Only this time it's more like a firing squad than a panel of judges. There are deep wrinkles in Henry's forehead as he says, "You. Are. *Not.* Fucking. Her."

It's one of those moments where time slows down so I know exactly how painfully long I hesitate in the space where I should be denying it.

"No. No, no, no," Henry says. "Jack, come on. You know better. This goes beyond shitting where you're eating. This is like—um—"

"I believe the phrase you're looking for is 'ejaculating where you've already conceived a child,'" Chase offers, prim as a middle-school sex-ed teacher.

None of us laugh. Because, let's face it, they have a point. What I'm doing is . . . messy.

"We made a pact," I say. "It's just while she's at my place."

Brooks squints. "Then what's the incentive for her to move out? She has a place to live, free child care, Jack the Magic Penis . . ."

Although I think I might be getting the better end of the deal, at least if the blow job she gave me Sunday night was any indication. Which, well, it was. Because it just gets sexier and sexier each time as we relearn each other.

Henry waves a hand in front of my eyes. "Yoo-hoo. Jack. You know where this leads. You're twenty-seven. You don't want this. You want to sow your wild oats and hit the road to head to Phoenix and—when was the last time you came out with us?"

"O'Hannihans. Last weekend."

"Weekend before last," Henry corrects.

"Come on. That's not that big a deal."

Henry waves his hands. "The point is, there are only two possible outcomes here. And they both suck. Outcome one: She never moves out. This becomes your life. Saying no to fun. Staying home with the kid. Missing once-in-a-lifetime road-trip opportunities. Outcome two: You tell her she's gotta leave so you can have your life back. And suddenly she's all, *But I thought this meant something to you.*"

"No," I say. "No, that's not going to happen. We were really honest with each other. Neither of us wants that."

Although I don't mention what I said to her Sunday night right before the epic blow job. About how she was welcome to stay as long as she needed to. Somehow I don't think that'll help my case with these guys. And it doesn't negate the fact that in the end, both Maddie and I know this is a short-term proposition.

"That's what she says," Henry says. "But like I said, what's not to like about her current setup?"

"Me," I say.

I get those six suspicious eyes on me again. I guess I

should be flattered that my friends think I'm such a sex machine that they can't imagine a woman walking away from me willingly.

"She knows me, and she knows how it is with me. She knows I'll hurt her in the end, and she's smart enough not to want that."

It's Chase's turn to squint at me. "It's not about *smart*," he says. "It's about how women get about sex. They can't help it. It's in their hormones. She'll say she's fine with the situation, but then when you kick her out, she'll act like it's a crime against humanity."

"Not Maddie," I say definitively.

Chase raises his eyebrows. "What about you?" he asks.

"What about me?"

"What if you're the one who doesn't want to walk away?"

Henry makes a sharp scoffing noise, but then, once again, three sets of eyes are trained on my face.

"Not gonna happen," I say. Because as good as things are between Maddie and me now, as much as I love climbing into her bed at night and being with someone who can match me and challenge me in every possible way sexually, I'm not the guy she wants to come home to. And that works fine for me, because I never wanted to be that guy, either.

Almost never, a quiet voice says in my head.

Shut up, I say back.

Brooks has gotten distracted again by making plans for Phoenix, but I can tell Henry's not listening as Brooks spins out lists of what we need to pack in the car, how we're going to party when we're down there, and who's going to control the music. He's still looking at me, with an expression on his face I just can't read.

23

JACK

"Where are you going?" Maddie asks, her eyebrows drawn together in confusion. It's Saturday morning, one week after our thunderstorm sex, and I am stuffing things into my backpack—peanut-butter-and-jelly sandwiches, water bottles, goldfish crackers (there are all kinds of things in my kitchen cabinets that were not there two weeks ago)—and she is standing next to me, looking at me like I'm stark raving mad.

"The aquarium," I say.

Her eyes get huge. "The *aquarium*?"

"With Gabe," I clarify. "So you can look at apartments if you need to."

"But—"

She appears to be at a loss for words, and I start to get pissed, because, what, is she going to be surprised every freaking time I do something for him? But then she says, "But *I'm* taking him to the aquarium."

I shake my head. "I don't think so."

"He asked me. This morning at breakfast."

"He asked *me*. Last night at bedtime."

"That—sneaky little— Gabe!"

He patters into the kitchen, still in his pajamas.

"Gabe, who's going to the aquarium today?" Maddie demands.

"I am!" he says, grinning ferociously.

"And who's going to the aquarium with you?"

"Mommy!" he says.

Maddie looks triumphant. I dig in for a battle, because he asked me first. But Gabe's grin grows and he says, "And Daddy! *Both*."

Son of a bitch. He's scheming.

Maddie's eyes meet mine. I see something there that makes me feel weirdly hopeful: confusion.

That makes two of us.

Of course, what Gabe doesn't know is that any scheming he can possibly do to get both his parents in the same room is nothing compared to what's been going on every night this week between Maddie and me. As soon as the kid is conked out, one of us jumps the other, and each episode is more epic than the last. It's like we're both trying to squeeze as many orgasms out of this situation as we possibly can before our time is up.

Not that Maddie's been looking terribly hard this week. After she didn't get a call back from the Ballard apartment landlord, she said she needed a few days to regroup. A few days turned into a few more days and about twenty more orgasms . . .

Neither of us has had much sleep this week.

But all those nighttime shenanigans are not the same thing as a two-parent outing with the kiddo. That feels . . .

It feels like something a family does.

Which should be impossibly weird, right? But I think I'm . . . I think I'm kind of okay with it.

Or maybe I'm just cruising to spend a day with her in that outfit: skin-tight jeans, nearly-knee-high low-heeled boots, and a black sweater that keeps slipping off one shoulder or the other to reveal a lacy black tank top underneath. I wonder how low that sweater could slip on that side? I bet if I told her she looked amazingly sexy, she'd say, "This old thing? It's just a sweater and jeans." Because that's how women are. They have no idea.

She's biting her lower lip, looking from me to Gabe.

"So you want to go?" she asks. "I mean, you actively want to?"

I get it. She's surprised I'd want to spend a free Saturday this way. And—I guess now that I think about it, it *is* a little surprising. A couple of weeks ago, I wouldn't have volunteered. I'd want to hang around, watching whatever games were on TV . . .

It occurs to me that I don't even know the schedule for this weekend's first-round March Madness games. When was the last time I didn't know the sports schedule? Or have money riding on a bracket?

The truth is, the idea of sitting around this weekend, watching college basketball—it doesn't appeal to me as much as it would have a couple of weeks ago. I mean, don't get me wrong. I'm not returning my big-screen TV. But breaking up a weekend of leisure with a couple of hours watching Gabe's eyes get huge as saucers in front of a tank full of otters or seals . . .

"I want to go," I say. "Like actually. Want. To. Go. So you

can go apartment hunting or whatever you want, or you can come with us."

I toss that off like it's nothing, but the truth is, I want her to come with us. And not just because she looks hot as fuck in that outfit and I'm still hoping that at any moment she'll have a wardrobe malfunction and I'll get to see what her tits look like under that lacy top. But because I don't just want to watch Gabe watch fish.

I want to watch Maddie watch Gabe watch fish.

I am so, so screwed.

24

———

MADDIE

Gabe loves the aquarium.

We visit the touch tanks first, and I boost him up so he can stroke his chubby little fingers through the anemones' tendrils and watch them close like pupils in bright sun. He runs his fingertips over the nubbly surface of the sea stars and draws back in delighted alarm when a wave swamps the tank.

Jack stands a little ways back, and when I look over at him, he's watching Gabe with unmasked affection. Something in my own chest contracts, hard and dangerous.

I'm not sure who I'm afraid for, Gabe or me or Jack.

After the tanks, we wander into the dark tunnel of the coral reefs, with their brightly lit windows. Gabe raises his arms over his head for a pick-me-up, and Jack lifts him up and points out the various creatures semi-camouflaged in the reef.

"Look," Jack says, pointing with Gabe's finger. "It's Dory."

We get treated to Gabe's recounting of the plot of *Finding*

Dory. Well, a mostly coherent version. There is a lot of stuff about the Hank the Septopus, and not all of it makes sense.

We wander through shorebirds, where Jack explains to Gabe that the funny-looking black and white and orange birds are puffins.

"There are puffins on my cereal," Gabe says.

"Yep," Jack says.

"Why?"

"Well, maybe because the cereal is puffy, and so they called it that, Puffins, and then they thought it would be cute to put a picture of a puffin on the box."

"Why?"

Jack slides me an alarmed look. I shrug.

"I guess they needed to put something on the box to make it fun to look at so people would want to buy it," Jack hazards.

"Why?"

I am struck by giggles. We've been in the "why" phase for a while now, but this is the first time I've heard Gabe treat Jack to a full-on encounter.

Jack narrows his eyes at me, a death look, and I try to rein in the giggles but give myself the hiccups instead. "You deserve that," he says in an undertone. To Gabe he says, "Because they need to sell the Puffins so they can make money."

"Why?"

Jack is starting to look panicked. "Because they're a business and that's the point of a business. Making money."

To both of our surprise and amusement, Gabe doesn't ask "why" again.

"You think he understood that explanation?" Jack asks me, as Gabe runs ahead up the ramp toward the next exhibit.

I shake my head. "No."

"So why'd he let me off the hook?"

"I think he sensed that you were in over your head."

He rolls his eyes and shoves me playfully. I shove him back. I barely rock him from his feet, and the lack of give is so satisfying I want to do it again. My hands want to explore more of that bicep muscle I just wrapped my fingers around, to follow the individual bands around his arm, into his shoulder, down to his sculpted chest. I let him walk a little ahead of me so I can get my mind off the subject of Jack's anatomy—this is a family show after all—but walking behind Jack turns out to be a terrible way to get my mind off the way he's put together, so I run to catch up to Gabe instead.

Gabe is enraptured by the underwater dome, the fish surrounding us 360 degrees, overhead and on all sides. He runs and darts and puts his hands on the glass like all the other toddlers. Jack and I stand a little way back, letting him move freely through the room, because there's really no trouble for him to get into except stepping on other people's feet, and everyone else in the room is either a kid or a parent, so I'm not too worried.

"I'm glad we did this," Jack says.

"You don't wish you were watching the game?" I tease.

He shakes his head, not matching my teasing, but watching Gabe through serious eyes. "I was scared of him," he says.

I don't get what he means at first.

"Of Gabe," he clarifies. "Especially when he was little. It always felt like I'd break him. So it was easier to let my mom and my sister do all the work."

I think my mouth falls open.

"And then, you know, they were good at it, they were the ones who knew how to do everything, so I kind of let it go on like that. But I'm glad. Glad I've gotten this chance. If what happened with you and Big Dick hadn't happened, I don't know what it woulda taken for me to spend more time with him."

I close my mouth and catch my breath and finally figure out what I want to say.

"I'm glad, too."

I wasn't sure this morning. About this whole trip. About the idea of all of us doing something together that felt like what a family would do together. Mom and dad and kid.

Every time Jack and I have been together this week, I've felt myself slipping a little further down a slope whose shape I know and whose pull I've never been able to resist. The only thing keeping it safe was that it was just sex.

But this isn't sex. And it isn't Jack's easy friendship, tossed at me like a fleece wrap at a football game. This day, this trip, is a promise I'm pretty darn sure Jack can't make.

Gabe comes running over and throws himself into my lap. "I'm hungry," he says. "I want goldfish."

It's lunchtime, so we take a break and get hot dogs in the cafeteria, Gabe kneeling up on his chair, so bubbly and bouncy, full of the stories of what he's seen, that I'm afraid he's going to fall over from sheer uncoordinated excitement. Jack is on alert too, poised with a hand that hovers near Gabe's squirmy little body, and I realize it's one of the first times I've been able to sit back and just watch because someone else is worrying about whether Gabe will fall off the chair.

Instead, Gabe reaches out and brushes too close to his

soda cup, and Jack lunges to catch it and knocks it over, a tsunami across the table and Gabe.

"*Sh—*"

Jack cuts the epithet off and rakes his gaze over the situation, taking stock. "You want the kid or the napkin run?" he asks, as Gabe, swamped in icy liquid, explodes into sobs.

I've never had a choice before. It's always been the screaming kid *and* the napkin run, and if I'm lucky some well-meaning wait staff or elderly woman with a grandmotherly air will blot at the puddle for a few seconds before wafting back to their own concerns.

Gabe has one hand knotted in Jack's shirt, so I run for napkins, and in a few seconds he has Gabe calmed down and I have the soda cleaned up.

I walk the wad of icy napkins to the trash can. As I turn back, I see that Jack is working Gabe out of his drenched shirt. He's already dug in the backpack for a change of clothes, which are draped over the back of the chair.

It takes my breath away, actually, how perfectly right the scene looks. And how I don't mind standing slightly outside it and watching Jack pull the new T-shirt over our son's head.

I could get used to this, I think, and then, my heart squeezing painfully in my chest, *Shit.*

25

JACK

Gabe doesn't stir as I lift him from the car seat and hold him loosely slung against my shoulder to carry him up to the house. "He's like a sack of rice," I whisper, as Maddie unlocks the door and lets us in.

I ferry him down the hall and deposit him in bed. Maddie tucks him in. The two of us stand there, staring down at him. He's so stinkin' cute with his face all pink and his hair all mussed, and I give in to the impulse to stroke his cheek with one finger. It's as soft as it looks.

I look up to find Maddie's eyes locked on my face. They're soft, too, and full of wonder, but as soon as she realizes I see her, her whole expression changes. It goes—stiff, I guess. Like she's shut down whatever's back there, behind her defenses.

I want her to let me in. To look at me that way, with all that vulnerability and need showing.

"This was a good day," I tell her.

"Yeah." I see it, just a glimmer of it, that softness. I want to reach out and stroke it like I did Gabe's cheek, but it's not a thing you can touch. It's like a wild animal that you have to lure out with quiet and gentleness. What happened between us, back then, it scared both of us bad enough that we're both like that, holding something back all the time.

Except—except when we have sex. I don't think either of us is holding anything back then.

She turns away from me, toward the door of Gabe's room. "I'm going to take a shower."

"You want company?"

Almost to the door, she turns back and regards me. Her lips twitch with amusement. Showering together is one thing we haven't done yet, mostly because at night we're busy crawling all over each other in bed, and during the day the one of us who isn't showering needs to be watching Gabe. "So, like, more of a 'getting dirty' shower than a 'getting clean' shower."

The way she says it brings my dick to immediate attention.

"Getting dirty on the way to getting clean."

I hear her breath catch.

"You don't mind that, do you, dirty girl?"

She whimpers her approval, biting her lip. Oh, that fucking lip. I cross the room, swoop her up, and carry her down the hall. She clutches fistfuls of my shirt and calls me a Neanderthal. The way she says it, I'm a hundred percent sure it's a compliment.

In the bathroom I strip her out of her clothes, my hands roaming everywhere. "The first couple weeks you were here you drove me crazy every time you showered," I tell her, kissing the corner of her mouth, her earlobe, her jawline, her throat, her tits. "I'd listen to the water run and all I could think about was you, naked and wet . . ." I groan. "I wanted to lick all that water off you . . ." I give her a demo, flicking my tongue over the whorls of her ear, along the line of her collarbone, down the slope of one breast until I can take the nipple in my mouth and treat it right.

Her knees buckle and I catch her, my arm looped tight around her, holding her up as I lavish all my attention on first one tight bud, then the other.

"You're still wearing all your clothes," she murmurs when I let her go, just long enough to turn on the shower.

I grab my T-shirt and tug it over my head, loving the hot way her eyes track my movements and her gaze slides down my torso to the button of my jeans. I put on a show with that button, slowly unfastening it and drawing down the zipper over my erection, which strains the fabric of my boxer briefs. I push my jeans and briefs down and stand naked before her, and she reaches out her hands, palms open, and begins to paint my body with big, lush strokes. Everywhere her hands touch there's a rush of heat and sensation, and it all gathers into my cock like sand draining to the apex of an hourglass. I'm wound tight already and we haven't even gotten under the water.

She steps into the shower and I follow her, loving her curves with my eyes—the flare of her hips, the heart-shaped curve of her ass, those generous tits, now drenched and dripping, the water streaming down the way I pictured, catching on the tips of her nipples and beading in her pubic hair and in her eyelashes. My mouth finds hers, my tongue licking against the wet silk of her lips and cheek and tongue like I'm still catching water droplets on her skin. She moans and leans into me, and the heat of her body with the heat of the water, touching me everywhere, is almost too much to take.

She reaches past me for the soap, slicks her hands with it, and winds her fingers against mine until we're both soapy. We touch each other like that, soapy and eager, almost desperate. She's so slippery under my hands, everything is slippery, and it's all I can do not to just plunge myself into her right now.

"No condom," I groan.

"Jack," she whispers. "If I said I have an IUD—"

"I'd say why the fuck didn't you tell me that before, woman!?"

She frowns. "You have to swear to me that you're clean...."

If her implied lack of trust burns at all, it gets swallowed in all the other heat around us, by how much in this moment I just want her no matter what. "I swear. I'm clean." I've got something to tell her that feels like a big deal, even though it shouldn't; it's just a statement of fact, it doesn't have to be all laden with meaning. But I have to catch my breath to get the words out, and they come out a little rushed, and cracked: "You're the last woman I fucked without a condom."

She takes a step back and holds me at arm's length for a moment, and I see that wide-open look in her eyes again, and I have that same insane feeling of wanting to reach out and touch it, touch *her* in some place that's beyond where my hands and fingers and tongue and lips can reach.

She takes a deep breath. "Okay. Okay." She closes her eyes, then opens them again and turns toward the wall.

She puts her hands against the tile, steps with one foot onto the ledge of the tub, and I don't wait for a written invitation. I cover her body with mine, our skin sliding soapy and slick and delicious against each other, and I thrust into her with one long stroke, she is so fucking wet and needy, and without the condom she is hotter inside than outside, hotter than the water raining down on us. We're wet from the shower and her generous slickness and the beads of pre-cum easing my way into her, from the way she's turned her head to catch my lips and lick hungrily into my mouth, from soap, water, sweat. My fingers weave through hers on the tile wall, the ceramic squares smooth and cold under our hands, her ass canted up to give me an angle that won't let me last more than a few seconds, her body like fire around mine and, now, gripping my dick tight as she comes, and nothing, no amount of willpower or desire to make this moment last forever could possibly stop me from shooting my own wet heat into her like it's just one more way the universe fits together.

26

MADDIE

Monday night, it takes me forever to pick my clothes for Tuesday. I fuss and fuss, trying things on and discarding the losers on the floor of the guest room.

"Wow," Jack says from the doorway. His gaze flicks from the pile on the floor to my nearly naked body—lace bra and panties—and back to the clothes before he settles on me and gives me a thorough visual going-over.

But I'm too sweaty and frustrated to melt under the heat in his eyes. "I don't have anything fun to wear out tomorrow night."

"Why does it matter? It's just Sienna and her girlfriends. Besides, you look sexy in everything. You're sexy in sweatpants."

"That's exactly why it matters. I can wear anything and you'll think it's sexy. But they're women. They actually have opinions about fashion."

And it's been a really long time since I had a group of girl-friends. People to hang out with, go out with.

"Just go like that."

"I'm serious. I want them to like me."

Jack sits on the edge of the bed. "They're going to like you, Maddie. Sienna already likes you. Always has. You don't have to dress to impress. But, okay. Show me what you've got."

I start re-trying on the least egregious of the rejects. No matter what I put on, he takes it off with his eyes and tell me it's sexy. Not helpful. And yet—

Really, really good for the ego.

"That," he says definitively.

I'm wearing a pair of bright-red satin leggings and an oversized white button-down.

"You need black boots."

I raise my eyebrows.

"What? Just because I'm a straight guy doesn't mean I'm not right about this."

I dig in the closet for my boots and pull them on.

"Fuck yeah," he says. "Now. Take it off."

The hard command in his voice goes straight to my core as a rush of heat. I kick the boots off and peel myself out of the satin pants, which I've miraculously spared, although my panties go into the corner in a damp wad.

"Boots back on."

I give him a *WTF* look and he looks right back at me, eyes flinty. I feel more moisture slick my sex. I reach for the boots and tug them back on. There something about it, the boots stiff and confining on my feet, the melting at my center, that amps me up even more, my nipples tightening, my breathing coming faster.

"Mmm," he says, eating me up visually. "Yeah. Just like that."

He leans back on the bed and just stares. Like I'm his own private porn movie. So, what the hell. I start unbuttoning the buttons of the white shirt, one by one. And then—because what's a strip tease without a dance?—I roll my hips a little. My core clenches around emptiness and I whimper.

"Yeah. Yeah."

His voice is rough, husky.

I run my fingertips across my collarbone, down over the slope of one breast, stroking lightly over the tip of one nipple through the lace of my bra. A little sigh escapes my lips, and Jack's hips buck.

"Touch that nipple again," he says. "But just like that. So lightly you can barely feel it."

I do.

"The other one."

There's moisture on my thighs now. I want him to come close and slip his fingers into it, spread it all around, find my hard clit at the center of the mess I've made of myself. But he doesn't. He just watches.

So I do it. I let the white shirt slip off my shoulders. My fingertips follow the upper outline of my bra, dip over the lace to flick a nipple, and then brush down the center of my chest, past the flirty little satin bow of my lingerie. Usually when I touch myself it doesn't feel as good as when Jack does it, but this time, with his eyes fierce and fixed on me, it's like it's his fingers. His hand behind my back, unhooking my bra, letting it drop, releasing my breasts with a last caress. The rough flat of his palm over my belly, his fingers dipping into my curls, smoothing my wetness everywhere.

Jack groans from the bed. His cock has raised a bulge in his jeans and my eyes want to linger there. But his hand cups it, covers it, so instead I watch the impatient, rough way he handles himself while I touch myself, gentle as a butterfly.

I raise my eyes from the spectacle at his fly and our gazes meet, spark. His eyes are so dark and hungry, almost angry in their intensity. And I want to push him harder, dare him more, make him crack. I raise my fingers to my lips, slide them in my mouth, and suck, hard, my eyes never leaving his —which means I can watch the heat flare there.

A moment later he's off the bed, kneeling at my feet, his mouth covering me as he coaxes wave after wave of orgasm out of me.

27

———————

MADDIE

Caverna is a new bar on Fifth near the theater, aptly dark and cozy, its walls lined with expensive bottles I've never heard of. I weave my way between closely packed tall tables and bar-height chairs to find Sienna and her friends with drinks in their hands. My Lyft got stuck in rush-hour traffic. I'd Lyfted to work so I could ride back to Revere Lake with Sienna and her friends after the show—not economical, but I didn't want to miss the post-show girl talk.

"Ladies," Sienna announces as I approach the table. "This is my friend Maddie. My nephew Gabe's mom."

I give her a hug. "Thanks so much for inviting me."

She hugs back, bony and fierce. "My pleasure. Maddie, this is Cora." She indicates a petite woman wearing a glittery tank and black leggings with a profusion of tight golden curls and a round face. She beams and waves. "Hey, Maddie."

"And this is Lani." Sienna opens her hand toward a tall woman with shiny black hair and a swervy figure—the kind that turns heads in bars even when it's not clothed, as now, in skinny jeans, a cream-colored halter top with a deep cleavage dive, and stilettos.

She's familiar. "Did you go to Revere Lake High?" I ask her.

Lani's gorgeous, smokily outlined green eyes research me carefully. It's unnerving. "I was a couple of years ahead of you. But yeah."

"I'm sorry, did we—I can't remember if we've actually *met* or if you're just familiar from the pass-in-the-hallway routine." Although I'm pretty good with names and faces; I think I'd know if we had met.

She shakes her head. Her gaze doesn't get any warmer. I feel like I've done something to piss her off without meaning to, but of course that's ridiculous. I've just met her. "I'm a friend of Jack's," she says.

She says it in a way that's carefully neutral, but something —call it female intuition—tells me that there's more to the story than "a friend of Jack's."

Then she seems to soften, and she sticks her hand out to shake mine. "Nice to meet you. And I love those leggings." She inclines her head down at my red satin.

"Cool boots, too," Cora adds, pointing at the boots Jack spec'd last night.

I blush. I will probably blush whenever anyone mentions these boots, possibly till I'm old, or dead.

The waitress comes by and asks what I want.

"You want one of these," Sienna says, pointing to her drink. "Bee's Knees."

The waitress confirms this. "It's the best drink. Sweet, but not too sweet."

"Sounds good. Thanks."

When she's gone, I incline my head toward Sienna and ask Lani, "So if you were two years ahead of me in school, and Sienna's three behind, how do you guys know each other?"

"Cora and I work for Lani," says Sienna, grinning.

"I own Cuppa, the coffee shop in town."

"Wow, cool," I say. "I haven't been in there yet, but I've heard it's got the best coffee in Revere Lake. How'd you get that gig?"

She tells me about buying it from the previous owner, who had driven it almost into the ground, and bringing it back from near-dead. Cora and Sienna were among her first employees, and she credits them with helping her figure out a vibe and a schedule that would work for tourists *and* locals. Lani smiles as she tells the story, her narrative picking up steam and energy until she's glowing with pleasure in her work. What came across as coldness or even anger earlier, I realize now, is just a little bit of shyness.

"Do you live in Revere Lake?" Cora asks me.

"Not permanently. Gabe and I are staying with Jack until I can find another place in the city."

"Oh, yeah," Lani says. "Jack told me that, right after you moved in. I ran into him hanging at O'Hannihans with Henry and a couple of other guys."

She's talking about the night he stayed out crazy late, then told me he was hanging with the guys and playing darts. Not "the guys and a really hot black-haired woman named Lani." *Not* that he's required to report anything to me.

That weird, hot feeling in the pit of my stomach—

Pretty sure that's jealousy.

But fuck me, there's no call for it. On the evening in question, Jack and I weren't even sleeping together. We'd had those two lapses of reason, the one on his couch and the one in his mom's kitchen, of course, but there was no interpretation under which we were together, even in the most rudimentary way.

And even if she told me that they'd slept together, I wouldn't have the right to be jealous. Because I have no claim on Jack. We've never said that what we're doing is anything other than scratching an itch—an incredibly intense itch, to be fair, but an itch. We've never even asked each other for exclusivity.

Most important, I've known all along who Jack is. I've known there are probably twenty women like Lani in his life. And the whole reason I said I wanted a firm end date on sex with Jack was because of this exact scenario. These moments would never stop coming. There would be one Lani after another—women who could mean nothing to Jack, or something, or everything. I'd have no way of knowing. One time after another I'd feel this domino series of emotions—jealousy, shame, anger at myself for feeling any of this over a guy I made a promise to myself almost five years ago not to love.

Death by a thousand cuts.

And whether he'd actually slept with Lani—or whoever —wouldn't even really matter. It was the fact that I believed he could have that would sink me.

Because he'd cheated on me once before, and once a cheater...

I could never live like this. With all the Lanis in the world just one casually uttered sentence away from breaking me.

No, I'd been right to keep him at bay, and when that became impossible, to at least put an expiration stamp on him. That way I might walk away from this with my pride and a couple of friendships intact.

"Maddie?"

Sienna's touching my sleeve.

"Sorry," I say. "I was . . . remembering something I forgot to tell Gabe's sitter."

Lani tilts her head to one side. Boy, those green eyes can drill into a face. I think she might see right through me.

"So, how's the search for a new place going?" Cora asks.

I tell them the whole story of my apartment travails, ending with the fact that the landlord from the Ballard place I'd wanted hadn't returned any of my five calls. I also told them I'd seen a few more places yesterday.

I don't say that I'd seen a place that wasn't too terrible but that I hadn't quite been able to make myself put in an application for. Because every time I tried to fill it out, I thought about how if it were accepted, it would mean never having sex with Jack again. Never feeling his mouth on mine, on my body, never putting mine on his, never feeling him inside me. That it would mean no more teasing, no joking, no talking dirty, no significant looks over Gabe's head. I wasn't quite ready, yesterday, to sign on the dotted line and give it all up.

"What's the story with your old apartment?" Sienna asks. "Jack hinted there was some drama."

I freeze.

"Bad story?" Lani asks, her eyes wise. I get the feeling she's got some bad stories of her own.

"Yeah, you could say that."

"Oh, damn, sorry—should have kept my mouth shut." Sienna wrinkles her face. "Don't feel like you have to tell us."

Cora and Lani are leaning on the table, faces sympathetic.

And I think it's because they're not pushing me to spill that I tell them what happened.

"Je-*sus*," Lani says, when I'm done. "I hope you kicked him in the balls."

Sienna pushes her drink one way, then the other. "I didn't — Wow, Maddie." When she raises her eyes to mine, they're full of apology, but I shake my head. She hadn't made me tell. I'd wanted to.

"I walked in on my boyfriend and a guy," Cora says.

I stare at her.

"Shit, I'm sorry, I didn't mean that in a one-up way."

I shake my head. "Not taken that way. I think getting cheated on is more a misery-loves-company thing."

"Tell her what happened," Lani commands.

Cora looks from her to Sienna, who nods.

"I came home from a book club and my boyfriend was on his knees in our living room, blowing the guy. I don't think he even saw me. The guy did, though. His eyes were *huge*. And then I just walked out. Lani and Sienna went back and picked up my stuff for me."

She beams at them, and Sienna touches her hand. "Damn straight we did."

It makes me smile.

"Sometimes when I tell that story, people are like, 'It's so great that he figured out who he really is,'" Cora says. "And sure, of course I'm glad he's out of the closet now. But cheating is cheating, you know? I bet he cheated on that blow-job guy, too . . . Once a cheater, always a cheater."

I think I flinch. I look up to find Sienna watching me. She looks away before I can.

"That's the fucking truth," Lani says. She turns to me. "Let us know if we can help with the apartment hunt." Then, in an echo of Sienna's gesture to Cora, she touches my hand. Just a brush, the barest gesture of support, but I feel about thirty seconds away from tears.

I like her. I like all of them. I'd like them to be my friends.

I don't want to be jealous of the women in my life. I don't want to see each of them as a potential competitor, to wonder if someday I'll walk in to find one of them on her knees in my living room.

I can't be with a guy I can't trust.

I need to move out of Jack's house. Like, yesterday.

28

MADDIE

We drop off Lani, then Cora. Sienna and I are left in the car alone as she turns toward Jack's house. Stripes of light from the streetlights carve across our faces and laps. She's taking the back route, off the main drag.

"Thank you again for including me. I had a great time. I loved the musical. But I also really loved your friends."

Both had hugged me tight as we said goodbye, and Lani had said, "Let's hang out again soon, okay?"

"I could tell they loved you, too," Sienna says lightly, but it doesn't feel light. It feels like a lot of bounty, something big to be grateful for. I'll never be glad for what Harris and Mia did, but I bet someday I'll look back at it as one of my life's best reminders that spring always comes after winter.

"Maddie?"

Sienna's tone is serious, and without knowing exactly what she's about to say, I feel myself hunkering down.

"I know it's none of my business . . ."

I clear my throat.

"And I know that's what people say when it's *really* none of their business . . ."

I'm quiet, unwilling to let her off the hook, but not quite ready to shut her down, either.

"What's going on with you and my brother?"

I think about saying, *nothing,* but can't, not quite. It's too big of a lie.

"It's just . . ." Sienna continues. "I see the way he looks at you. I've never seen him look that way at anyone. And I saw your face when Lani was talking about him. Maddie, you've got to know there's nothing between them."

"Nothing?" I challenge.

Sienna sighs. "I mean, they've gone a round or two. Or, I don't know, twenty."

My gut goes sours with jealousy. And Sienna takes her eyes off the road at that exact moment and catches the expression on my face.

"My point," she says quietly. "But, Maddie, it's just convenience sex with them. They'd both tell you that straight out if you asked."

I hunch my shoulders. Maybe it's the words *convenience sex,* which I know she means to make me feel better, but—

How different is that from what he's doing with me? I mean, how much more convenient does it get than having your fuck buddy live in your house?

"I probably— I don't think I should be talking about this with you." She puts a gentle hand on my arm. "I like to think I know my brother better than anyone. I like to think I understand what he's gone through and what matters to him. And —you can't tell him I told you this, Maddie."

For a split second I'm sure she's going to say, *He's never going to be the guy you want him to be.*

Instead, she says, "I think he's in love with you."

Something inside me, rusty with disuse, tries to grind to life. And that little flare of hope scares me so much that I declare, "It's lust."

I say it so flatly that it comes out harsh, so I try to soften it: "It's crazy-good sex—"

She puts a hand to her temple like she's blocking me out.

"Sorry. But you asked!"

"I did. Which I might live to regret. But I can't watch two people I care about—three, counting Gabe—dance around each other and go spinning off in different directions. So I will put on the big-girl pants and let you talk to me about my brother's sex life. 'Crazy-good sex.'" She winces, visibly. "And so you think it's just lust."

"I know it is. It's—" It's almost painful to say it, but I do. "Just 'convenience sex.'"

"For you?"

"For both of us. It'll burn itself out, like last time."

She turns onto Jack's street. Pulls up in front of his house. Parks the car and half turns in her seat to look at me. Her gaze is sharp, knowing. "Last time?"

"None of your business," I mutter. I reach for the car door.

"It isn't. I get that." Her voice is gentle.

I pull my hand back. And sit there, staring straight through the windshield, seeing nothing.

"What happened?" she asks quietly.

My period was five days late, and I peed on a stick and a small pink plus sign appeared. It was that simple. There was no denial, no days of delay while I lied to myself about why I was so nauseous or tired or my breasts were swollen or I was peeing all the time. I stared at the white plastic stick numbly for a few minutes, and then went and lay down on my bed and fell asleep. Not because I was so tired, but because I couldn't face reality. Not yet.

I was going back to school in two days, and that was bad enough. It was bad because I was in love with Jack Parker and I hadn't found a way to tell him. And I was pretty sure that even if I did tell him, it wouldn't matter. Two nights before I took the pregnancy test, after he turned my world upside down for the umpteenth time, while I was still lying next to him trying to recover my breath and my equilibrium, while I was thinking, *This. This is how it's supposed to be,* he'd said, "I am going to miss this after you're gone."

Not, "I'm going to miss you so much."

Not, "I'm going to miss this until I get a free weekend and can drive down to Eugene so we can do it again."

Not even, "I'm going to miss this until you get home to visit and we can knock boots like old times."

Just, "I'm going to miss this after you're gone."

So even before the stick showed me its little pink secret, it was going to be one of the hardest things I'd ever had to do, telling Jack the truth. Going to him and saying, "For me, this isn't just sex. This is about feeling like when I'm with you, I'm completely safe and happy and exactly where I'm supposed to be. It's about feeling like we fit together. Like I see the best in you and you see the best in me. Like being together makes us both better people than we could ever be alone."

But I was going to do it. I was going to say it because I couldn't imagine having to live with not saying it. With never knowing if he felt the same way.

Once the stick betrayed me, though, it became a whole different truth I was going to have to tell. And I knew exactly how Jack Parker felt about fatherhood because he'd told me, after we'd run into a high school friend of his who was about to become a father.

"That poor fucker," he'd said, after the guy left.

"He seems happy about it," I hazarded. He'd been talking about shopping for a stroller with the same passion other guys talked about cars.

"He's too young."

"And that's what bothers you?"

"I just don't see him—he's not ready to give this up."

He indicated O'Hannihans around us, the sex-drenched scene, seeming to encompass me, even *us,* in his gesture.

"Are you sure you're not just projecting?" I teased.

"Yeah, well, that," he said, grinning at me.

"So—no fatherhood in your future plans?"

I asked it as casually as I could.

"Might be for some guys, but it's not for me. Not the way I was raised, not with my dad. Just seems like shitty odds I'd be any better at it than he was."

I'd left it at that. If I felt a twinge of grief, I shrugged it off because, after all, there wasn't anything at stake.

And now here I was, on my way to his apartment with information he didn't want, poised to shit all over his happy bachelor life, and without even any assurance from him that I was worth the five-hour drive to Eugene, Oregon, let alone a life sacrifice of epic proportions.

But I was doing it. I was going.

I parked my car in one of the visitor spaces and looked up at the balcony that contained his door. I was gathering my courage and still trying to figure out how to get it all out in an order that made sense. Would I tell him first how I felt about him, and then present the fact that I was pregnant? Or should I lead with the big news? Even now, five years later, I don't really know the answer. Either way, it felt like an ambush.

As I hesitated, the door to Jack's apartment opened and someone stepped out. It was a woman. I didn't recognize her. She had shoulder-length glossy blond hair and wore a short, emerald-green A-line dress. She was made up in a showy but not cheap way, and she was carrying something in one hand.

I observed all these details dispassionately, one at a time, just the way I've reported them.

Despite the glossiness of her hair, a bit of it had gone askew and was clinging, staticky, to her cheek. The makeup under one eye bore a smudge.

The item in her hand was her high-heeled sandals. And something else.

She came down the steps along the side of the building and crossed not too far from my car. Close enough that I could see what the other thing was that she held in her hand.

It was her bra, balled up but not fully contained by her fist. I could see one strap with its unmistakable metal slides, and a bit of emerald lace.

My breath stopped for a moment. I think my heart might have paused, as if it, too, were waiting to see what would happen next. And then the world and all the implications of what I'd just seen rushed in like water into a collapsing levee, and I almost choked on it.

I took a breath—shallow but sufficient—and shored up the levee with all the emotional sandbags I had at my disposal.

Then I started my car and pulled out of my parking spot.

29

———————

MADDIE

"So, that was it? You just drove away?"

Sienna sounds angry.

"I wanted to," I admit. "I never wanted to talk to him again, let alone have the conversation I needed to have with him. But I couldn't do it. The same thing that made me go there in the first place, knowing I wouldn't be able to live with myself if I didn't give him a chance to—"

I couldn't quite finish. I couldn't quite name what it was I'd wanted Jack to do. Claim me. Claim *us.*

Even that afternoon, Gabe was there with me. I didn't know his name yet. I hadn't felt the softness of his skin or the clutch of his little mouth at my breast, I hadn't giggled at his twisted syntax or cried because his case of the stomach flu hurt *me,* but he was already on board and part of how I thought of myself and my life. And even if I could have walked away from Jack and the sight of that scrap of emerald lace betrayal, I couldn't deprive Jack and Gabe of each other without at least trying.

"I made it as far as the street and then I pulled back into

the parking lot and got out of my car. I went upstairs and knocked on the door. He opened it. I was trying not to cry, and I guess that and my body language told him what he needed to know. He said, 'You—saw her—leaving?'

"I nodded. And then I said, 'Look, Jack, you don't owe me anything. We didn't promise each other anything. But I should tell you. I'm pregnant.'"

"He said, 'Shit.'"

It still felt like a body blow. I might have even winced in the retelling.

"That's what he said?" Sienna screeches. "Oh, that—" She throws her arms up. "Jesus, Jack."

"So I said, 'I get that this isn't in your plans. I get that fatherhood isn't your thing.'

"'If you didn't believe me about that before, you should now,' he said.

"I was having trouble talking by that point. I just wanted to get out of there. I said, 'I just want you to know, I'm going to have the baby. And you're welcome to be involved. If you want. To whatever extent.'"

I have to pause to steady my breath. "He shrugged."

Sienna closes her eyes.

"He said he'd give it some thought. Those were his exact words. 'I'll give it some thought.'"

It's so quiet I can hear both of us breathing, my breath ragged from emotion.

"But—" Sienna opens her eyes. "You didn't tell him you were in love with him. You didn't tell him all those things about how you fit together and made each other better people—you didn't say any of that."

I shake my head.

"And you didn't ask him if he'd slept with her. The woman. With the shoes and the bra."

I understand what she's driving at. She's hopeful that this story I'm telling holds a secret, a revelation, a big misunderstanding that redeems her brother and, in the process, a relationship. But this isn't that story. There's no happily-ever-after in the story of me and Jack and Gabe.

I take a deep breath. "Yeah, I did. I told him to let me know what he came up with after 'giving it some thought.' And then I turned to let myself out. But at the last minute, I turned back. I said, 'Did you have sex with her?'

"I didn't want to ask it. I was ashamed of myself for cracking like that, for being pathetic and jealous. So of course, I did the worst possible thing. I started to cry."

"Oh, Maddie," Sienna says, and her eyes are bright with unshed tears.

"He got this look on his face, like—like—a trapped animal. He said, 'Maddie. This is who I am. If it wasn't her, it would be someone else. You know that, right? You're really great, you really are, but I'm nobody's father and nobody's husband.'"

"Oh, *Jack*," Sienna groans.

We sit for a moment in silence. I feel exhausted, spent, from telling the story. She has moved closer to the door and turned away from me, so I can see only half her face, in shadow.

When she turns back, her face is eager, almost desperate. She grabs my arm. "People change," she whispers. "That was five years ago. He's older. He's wiser. Don't you think it's possible he's a different man now?"

I get it. I get what she wants. For her brother, maybe even

for me. What so many people want: love and trust. Family. Home.

I want it too. But . . .

I think about Lani and my jealousy.

I think about Mia's skirt and Harris on his knees, about those moments when you stand in place and the whole world turns itself around you, so you lose your orientation and aren't sure if the sky is even still up.

I think about Cora, watching her boyfriend swallow a stranger's cock in their living room.

I put my hand over Sienna's, touch her fingertips until they unfurl from my skin and I can draw my arm back. I wrap both my arms around myself for warmth. "That thing that Cora said. *Once a cheater, always a cheater.* Most of the time, I think it's true. But not always. I think some people cheat for reasons and when those reasons aren't true anymore, they stop. So—yeah, I mean, I think it's possible. I think some people change. I even think Jack could change. I just—"

I gulp air. I think about the night that Mia came to the house, what Jack said to her, to himself: *You idiot. It doesn't matter if she forgives you. She'll never trust you again.*

"I just don't think *I* can change."

30

———————

JACK

Wednesday evening I come home to find Gabe playing with Legos on the living room floor and Maddie sacked out on the couch. Her dark hair is fanned out around her, her mouth is slightly open, which makes me want to kiss it, and her cheeks are pink.

"Hey, bud," I say, ruffling Gabe's still baby-soft hair. "Your mama looks tired."

He tilts his head, gives her a thoughtful look, and returns to the structure in his hands.

"How 'bout you and I cook for her?"

He's on his feet instantly. "Yeah!"

"I'm not as good a cook as your mama, though."

He doesn't care. He's racing toward the kitchen and trying to get the step stool out of the pantry. I stop him before he drops it on his head or pinches his fingers, carry it into the kitchen, and set it up at the end of the counter. He scrambles up.

"So, here's what I got, dude. I make mean bacon, egg, and

cheese sandwiches. You like bacon, egg, and cheese sandwiches?"

"What dat?"

"It's like grilled cheese with bacon and a fried egg in it."

He shakes his head violently.

"You like grilled cheese, though."

He nods.

"And you like bacon."

He nods.

"And you like fried eggs."

He nods.

"Okay. So I'll make you a grilled cheese sandwich and a fried egg and you can have your bacon on the side."

He jumps up and down approvingly on the stool. I catch his arm just in time to prevent him falling off. "No jumping on the stool, bud."

"Why?"

"Because you could fall and hurt yourself."

"Why?"

To buy myself time to consider the answer, I go to the fridge and take out the bacon, egg, cheese, butter, and bread. For whatever reason, as crazy as it may seem, I feel compelled to answer his questions as accurately as possible. Maybe because my dad would have said something like, *Can't you see I'm fucking busy?*

"Okay, see, there's this thing called gravity."

"Why?"

I get out the griddle and start it heating. I put a couple of slices of toast in the toaster but don't push them down yet. Gotta get the timing right. I'm thinking about what I remember from school. "Anything that"— I can't say "has mass" because he'll have no idea what that means—"is big enough will pull other big things close to it. So the earth, which is what we're standing on, is really big and round, which means it pulls on us, which is what keeps us close to it. It's what keeps us standing on the floor instead of floating up to the ceiling. But it's also what makes you fall and hit your head if you aren't careful about where you're jumping."

Gabe is staring raptly at me. "C'we float to the see-wing?"

"Um, no."

"Why?"

I butter the griddle. "Because gravity pulls us down."

"Why?"

"And . . . this went on for some time," intones a voice from the doorway. Maddie is standing there, looking sleep-mussed and flushed and beautiful. She surveys the room.

"You're making me dinner," she says wonderingly. Her face has softened into that tender expression that makes me want to wrap her in my arms and kiss her.

"Well, don't celebrate yet. It's breakfast for dinner."

"I don't care. I don't have to cook. You are a god among men."

I would like her to keep looking at me like that. Like I really am a god. Like I can do no wrong, like I've never done wrong in her eyes.

Fuck it—I set down the butter and the knife, cross to her, and kiss her. Her mouth softens sweetly under mine, and I have to remind myself that we have an audience. I remove my lips from hers unwillingly. I'm a little dazed. And something else it takes me a moment to name: happy.

"Why?" Gabe persists.

"It's just what gravity *does*. It's what makes everything fall down instead of up." In this mood, with Maddie beaming at me with affection and approval, I could answer his questions all day long.

"No, Daddy, why you kiss Mommy?"

"Because Mommy has gravity." I take one of her hands and dance around her in a circle. She gives me a *you're crazy* look, but she's smiling. "I am in her orbit. She is pulling me in."

"She big?"

Maddie plants her hands on her hips and raises her eyebrows.

"Only in the best possible way," I tell Gabe, waggling one eyebrow at Maddie, who sticks her tongue out at me.

"Why?" Gabe asks.

"I'm going to save that one for when you're older, bud," I tell him.

I spiral toward her and plant one more swift kiss on her lips.

When I pull back, her eyes are full of warmth. And something else.

Sadness.

"Jack. I have some—news."

I know what she's going to say before she says it.

"I got the apartment."

"Which?"

She looks away, at the floor. "The one I looked at the weekend before last, the night your mom and your sister were here playing Hearts. The one I actually liked."

"Then that's—that's great."

Never have words been spoken with more force and less conviction. And she knows it. Our eyes meet, and all the giddy happiness I'd been feeling a few minutes earlier leaches out of me. We just stand there, looking at each other. Gabe, too, is quiet, watching us both with big eyes.

"So, when?"

"This, um, this weekend. Her other tenant fell through, and she asked if I could be in ASAP—she really doesn't want it vacant."

"Wow," I say. *Jesus.* This weekend. As in, a few days from now. "If it feels too soon, you don't have to take this one. I mean, you could wait and see what comes up."

"I told her I'd take it, Jack."

That shuts me up.

She looks away, toward the corner of the kitchen, her gaze far off. Then her eyes snap back to my face and she shakes her head. "I had to take it. I looked for weeks without finding anything. If I didn't take this one, I just felt like, who knows when another one will come up."

"There's no rush."

But she's shaking her head. "This can't just be an indefinite thing, Jack. We both know that's not a good idea."

In other words, *I'd be okay with continuing our bonkfest for another few weeks, but this—this whatever-it-is between us— can't be permanent.*

Which—that's what I want, too, right? There's no percentage on this lasting past another few weeks. I mean, what's my past track record for longest chunk of monogamy?

Oh, right. The last time I was sleeping with Maddie.

I wince.

"Daddy, you sad?" Gabe asks.

His eyes are big and concerned. I have no idea how much he hears or understands, but I do know it's our job as adults not to let him worry about anything, especially not this messy territory Maddie and I have ducked into. "I'm happy! Your mama found a great place for you guys to live!"

"We should talk about this later," Maddie says, aiming a significant look in Gabe's direction.

I nod, while Gabe grins maniacally back at me, and I realize it's an exact replica of the too-cheerful smile I've plastered on my own face. I adjust the size of my smile, then give up and let it slip off my face. I busy myself assembling the rest of our dinner sandwiches, frying up bacon, flipping eggs, breaking yolks so they'll cook through, melting cheese slices on top of them, slapping sandwich components on bread. Having something to do is soothing, but it doesn't stop the weird, unfamiliar ache that's forming in the pit of my stomach.

We sit and eat. It's so quiet I can hear Gabe's chewing, since he hasn't quite figured out the whole close-your-mouth-while-there's-food-in-it thing. He's excited about his sandwich, and his egg, and his bacon, although he still flatly refuses to try the three together.

Whatever. What do I care if he's a picky eater? I only have to deal with his eating every third weekend.

Henry and Brooks will be thrilled.

I'll be back to my normal prowl.

I can go on the Phoenix trip.

I don't feel even an iota of excitement about any of it. Not even about being sprung for the road trip. Not that I don't think it would be fun. Of course it would be great. But if I had to miss it for another weekend with Maddie, I would happily do it.

"How was work?" Maddie asks.

Work was a whole new level of clusterfuck. I'd forgotten all about it as soon as I'd walked through the door and found Maddie sprawled out on the couch and Gabe sitting on the floor with his Legos. Their faces—and Gabe's eagerness to cook dinner with me—had put today's bullshit right out of my mind. Now it's clamoring back. The wrong kitchen sink ordered, screwed-up measurements on the countertops. I'd asked my boss a while back to double-check the orders and the measurements, and what I'd gotten for my efforts was a reaming out. *Stick to power tools and let me handle the tricky stuff.*

When it all went south today, he told me that I'd let too many things slip through the cracks; one more and I'd have to look for a new job.

Even then, I hadn't been as upset as you'd think. As if I was insulated from that crap by knowing I'd get to come home to Maddie and Gabe; that however much horse manure my boss could shovel, it couldn't dampen the pleasure of seeing their eyes light up when I walked in the front door.

But that wouldn't be a thing, not after Friday.

"Work was fine."

She gives me a long look that contains multitudes. I shrug.

"'Fine'?" she demands.

"Whatever. It is what it is."

I don't want to tell her the story of my day for so many reasons. I don't want her eyes boring into my head, the way she looks at me like she can see through everything. I don't want her to tell me I'm more than he says I am, that I deserve better, that I could start my own business or—whatever. I don't want her to fuss or worry or ask me what I'll do if I lose this job. I don't want her to talk to me at all, because—

I don't want her to cheer me up.

After Friday, she won't be around to cheer me up.

She's not my family. And she doesn't live here.

31

JACK

As I'm trying to make my exit from his bedroom, Gabe sits up and tosses off his covers for, I don't know, probably the eighth time. "Daddy . . ."

"Lie down, bud." I say it gently, but a fist tightens in my chest. I'm losing patience with him. I want to get back to the living room to talk to Maddie about the apartment thing. I want to tell her she needs to postpone it a week or two. I mean, what's the difference to the landlord whether they move in now or in two weeks? We can go over there on a daily basis and check up on the place, or whatever it takes to ease the landlord's fears about it being vacant for a little longer.

And that will give me more time to convince her that—

That what?

That I've changed? That I've become the kind of guy who commits? A father? A husband?

Like my father, who was the worst kind of father and the worst kind of husband? Hateful, and then . . . gone.

What kind of an asshole would I be if I selfishly kept

Maddie near me, knowing how little potential I have to make her happy?

"I need a drink of water, Daddy." Gabe slides his legs out from under the sheets toward the side of the bed.

I steer them back and pull up the covers. "You had a drink. If you drink more, you'll have to go to the bathroom in the middle of the night."

"But I'm thirsty." He kicks his legs out against my hands, catching me in the wrist. It hurts surprisingly much for an injury inflicted by a preschooler. A little twist of irritation rises up.

I crush the emotion and get him one more small cup of water. He doesn't even drink it. He just takes it and puts it on the bedside table, which irritates me even more. He was manipulating me. I was manipulated by a four-year-old.

I make my voice calm and say, "Okay. Now time for sleeping."

"I'm not sleepy."

I take a deep breath, rebuild the wall holding back the wave of anger. "It's bedtime, bud. You need to lie down. Here. I'll put the radio on."

I reach over and dial his radio until I pull down an a.m. station that's broadcasting a basketball game. He settles onto the pillow, and I breathe a sigh of relief.

"Sleep tight, bud."

"G'night, Daddy."

I kiss his forehead.

In the living room, Maddie is standing by the fireplace.

"He down?"

"I think. He was tough. He didn't want me to leave."

Maybe he doesn't want to leave.

I don't want him to leave.

I don't want you *to leave.*

"Maddie, about the apartment."

She turns an agonized face to me. "Jack, please."

"Maddie, I don't think you should take it. I mean, things are . . ." I cast around for a way to say what I'm feeling. "This thing between us. It's not—"

It's not just sex.

It's not like anything I've ever experienced.

It's not something you can walk away from or throw away.

"It's not *over* yet."

That wasn't right. That wasn't what I was trying to say. I open my mouth again, but she breaks in.

"Jack, we agreed. We said this was just until I got an apartment."

I want to reach out and haul her into my arms. Kiss her until she gives up resisting and says the thing I'm trying to say but can't. That we need to give this time. That we need to give each other another chance.

"Maybe we were wrong."

"Jack, I can't do this again. It hurt too bad the first time. I can't put my heart out there again and feel hopeful and then have you decide you're not this guy. That this isn't a thing you can do or commit to. That you've got an itch to scratch—"

I open my mouth to tell her. To tell her how fucking wrong she is, about everything. My head and chest are full of words, scrabbling to get out.

"Daddy, I can't sleep."

All the words I'd been trying to corral, the ones swirling around, clawing for purchase, gather themselves into one dark funnel cloud.

"Gabe—" I say, and then stop. Because I thought I had it sealed down, but when his name comes out of my mouth, I hear it. My irritation, my anger.

I hear my father.

Jack, you little fucker! You're supposed to be in bed! How hard is it? Just get your ass down the hall—

Coming closer, his face purple, his mouth twisted.

I'm lost, for a split second, in the past.

"Jack," Maddie says quietly. "I've got this."

She reaches out a hand to touch the muscle at the corner of my jaw, which throbs from how hard I've locked it down.

Slowly, responding to the warmth and softness of her touch, my muscles unlock. The anger goes out of me.

But it was there.

He's there, inside me.

And she saw it.

Not that she needed to see it. She's always known it was in there.

With one quick glance at me, Maddie hustles Gabe out of the living room and down the hall.

I stand in the living room, my arms limp by my sides. My mind is blank, except for one thought. *My mother used to do that. Try to keep me out of my father's hair so he wouldn't, couldn't lash out at me.*

Maddie comes back in. "If he comes out again, I've got him." She looks at me warily, the way you watch a strange dog. "You okay?"

I nod.

"It's frustrating, right, trying to get him to bed? It can make a saint crazy."

And if you have a lit fuse buried in your genes...

"Maddie."

She gets this look on her face, like she's gearing up for another fight.

"You're right."

Her eyes are big with surprise. That wasn't what she thought I was about to say.

"It's better this way. It's better if you guys move out now."

She hesitates, as if she's about to say something.

When she opens her mouth, what she says is, "Okay."

32

———————

MADDIE

There's a soft knock at my door.

"Come in."

I know it's Jack. And I'm both surprised and not surprised that he's here. The way things ended earlier this evening—it didn't feel finished. He agreed it had to be over between us, but—

I knew we still needed to say goodbye, somehow.

He looks uncertain. I'm not sure I've ever seen him look like that, not even when he was doing something for Gabe that I knew was outside his comfort zone. Even then he was all bravado, like *Facebook evidence to the contrary, I've got this Dad Business down.* But right now he just looks tentative.

"Hey," I say, and I reach for his hand.

"You have the new place. I wasn't sure if this was still allowed."

It makes me laugh, but it also humbles me. Jack is a guy who's never in his life hesitated to push the limits of what's allowed. And here he is, asking me if this is okay. And I understand that he means that if it isn't, he won't try to convince me or seduce me. He's never taken anything from me I didn't want to give, and I've tried my hardest never to ask anything from him that he couldn't give. I guess that's what makes us such good friends, when all is said and done.

I feel such a wave of warmth and affection for him right now. It's so much quieter than the sexual heat that usually steers us through these situations, but in a way, it's much more intense, too. Like when someone speaks softly in a loud room and everyone quiets down to hear.

"We made the rules," I say. "So we say if this is allowed."

He still hesitates, so I kneel up, tug him closer to the bed, and draw his head down for a kiss. The kiss is like the way I feel: quiet and intense. It resonates in the smallest parts of me —a quivering where I'm put together.

"Maddie," he says.

He kisses me again, his tongue delicately searching me out, his breath warm on my lips, the scent of his skin and the heat of his body inches away as strong in my senses as his mouth on mine.

He says my name again. And each time it's like a measurement, a notch up from where we were, the heat and excitement mounting in my body while we keep on kissing like there's nothing frantic going on in the air molecules between us. Except my body keeps drifting closer to his, until my breasts touch his chest and he groans like I've burned him and slips a hand behind me and slides me down onto the bed, covering me. And then he keeps on kissing, but now his weight is on me, his thick erection between my legs, and I think I am going to dissolve. I am dissolving. But he's holding me together with kisses and touches, defining the edges of my body so I can't lose track of it completely, and I feel this surge of wild gratitude that makes absolutely no sense.

I pull at his clothes and he pulls at mine, and we have to get a hold of ourselves and stop the yanking and cooperate so we can get them all off, bit by bit, sinking back into the bed, back into each other, skin now bare along our lengths. So much skin touching, so hot, I'm luminous all over from it. My breasts feel tight and tender between us and I find his hand and bring it up, bring his fingertips to my nipple, and he makes a raw, broken sound and slides down to take the nipple in his mouth. I moan and arch, and his fingers find me slick between my legs, teasing lightly. Then he replaces his fingers with his cock, gliding it through my sex and over my swollen clit. I gasp, and he does it again, a slow, luxurious back-and-forth that makes me whimper.

"Inside," I beg.

He obliges, with that same slow tease I've come to know so well now: just the head, while he watches my face, then a little more, until I arch my hips up and steal the tease away from him, thrusting to take all of him in one good stroke. His turn to groan.

He props himself on his arms and gazes down at me, face soft, eyes dark. It's a different way he's watching now, though, than before. Like he's trying to understand something in a language he doesn't quite know, like he's trying to read something behind my expression. More tender than intense. His hand comes up and touches my cheekbone, soothing, smoothing, so gentle that tears spring into my eyes. Where we're joined below he thrusts rhythmically, slowly, pressing so deep the tension tugs tight and I ruck up against him, a fist of tension forming in my lower belly, drawing inward on itself. And then, still reading my face, he slows down even more, and I feel myself start to come, a long buildup like falling and falling and falling into the brilliant center of pleasure.

"Oh," he says. Just that. And closes his eyes. He rests his cheek against mine, and he thrusts deep one more time and holds still, his body rigid, his breath faltering. "Ohhh. Ohhh-hh." As if it's too good for words, fine and smooth and perfect, this one last time.

I don't let him see the tear that rolls down my face and slides quietly into my hair.

33

MADDIE

If I keep myself busy enough, I won't be able to think.
Or feel.

If I work all day, cook dinner for Gabe and me, pack our stuff, and fall into bed exhausted, I won't be awake long enough to lie there, wondering. Wishing.

Or that's the theory, anyway.

The reality is that it's 1 a.m. on Friday night, the night before our move, and I'm not asleep. I'm wide awake, and I'm hyper-tuned to the sounds in the house.

Last night, Jack went out with his guy friends. He didn't even come home from work. He just texted to ask if Gabe and I would be okay on our own and to say that he had plans with the guys. I texted back, *We're fine.* And of course we were. Gabe and I made spaghetti and had a delicious meal together, followed by a lovely, peaceful storybook bedtime.

Gabe only asked me about ten thousand times where Daddy was. And each time felt only a little bit like a barbed arrow in my heart.

Despite the pain, I wasn't at all tempted to change course. My sadness only made me more convinced that I was doing the right thing, because the longer Gabe and I live under Jack's roof, the harder it will be to say goodbye. And the harder it will be for Gabe to understand that this situation is only temporary, that it has to be temporary.

Of course, Gabe can't really understand, but maybe someday when he's older I can explain. Not that I have any idea what I'll say. It's heartbreak city, no matter how you spin it. I just have to have faith that in the end, Gabe will know he has a mother who loves him more than anything and a father who, even if he will never be a TV-perfect dad, loves him too.

I don't doubt that Jack loves Gabe, not at all. I've seen it in his face and his actions, in the time Jack has spent with Gabe, the way he's learned the little details of the bedtime routine and improvised some of his own. In the photos he texts me, the way he leapt into action the other day at the aquarium, his willingness to cook with Gabe and get down on the floor and play with Legos.

I don't even doubt that Jack loves me, in his own way. I just know that it's not the way that he needs to in order to want to blow up his bachelor existence for us. And in my own way, despite my sadness, I totally get that.

Still, I am lying in bed right now thinking about what Jack's doing, and it's making me crazy. I've pictured him and the guys in Jack's truck on the way to O'Hannihans, plotting their approach. I've pictured him jumping down from the driver's seat, striding into the bar with his alpha-confident swagger. Turning heads as he walks in. Catching someone's eye. Buying her a drink, chatting her up, making her feel like she's the center of his universe. And she probably is, for those few minutes—or even days or weeks.

The woman I picture, the one who catches his eye, is Lani, of course. Wearing something outrageous, raven hair down around her shoulders, greeting him with her beautiful wide smile.

Have you ever noticed how the absolute worst jealousy is what you feel toward people you genuinely admire? So I'm basically just torturing myself by imagining him with her, because who could blame him? She's fun and gorgeous and sexy and smart and I hate her right now and I hate myself for it.

I understand why people talk about being "consumed" by jealousy, because it really does feel like some big monster has me in its slobbery jaws.

I know that no matter what I do, I won't be able to stop wishing Jack were here with me instead of out with —whoever.

Only time will cure that.

I know that no matter what I do, I won't be able to stop loving him. Probably even time won't cure that, but it will blunt it, and maybe I'll find someone else I genuinely care about. For the time I was with Harris, I didn't miss Jack so much. Sure, I compared them, even if I didn't want to admit to myself that I was doing it, and even if sometimes I outright lied to myself. Like, *Harris is such a dependable guy. If I'd gotten pregnant by someone like that, things would be different. Sure, there wouldn't have been so much passion, but there also wouldn't have been so much drama. And that's good, right? Less drama. That's what adult women should want in their lives.*

I know I'll meet someone else eventually.

I also know, deeper than bone, that it will never be like it is with Jack.

I glance at the clock, at the numbers that now say 1:11, and resign myself to being okay with that.

JACK

I don't know how to describe Saturday.

It's like nothing's changed and everything's changed. Like we go through all the same motions we always do, but the guts have been scooped out. Like my own guts have been scooped out.

I make pancakes, to fortify Gabe and Maddie for the move. And Gabe stands on his stool and helps. Maddie comes in and smiles at us, but it's a hollowed-out smile. I smile at her, but it's only on the outside of my face.

The last two nights I've gone to O'Hannihans and drunk a lot of Jameson. I've listened to Henry, Chase, and Brooks sling bullshit over my head and been grateful that they haven't demanded to know what the fuck is wrong with me.

I'm pretty sure they know. And like the excellent friends they are, they haven't said a word.

Meanwhile, I've worked hard not to be an asshole, because right now all I want to do is sulk and lash out. But I've been pretty good. I haven't yelled at my crew or spewed nastiness at my boss or gotten in a fight with my friends. I haven't driven while under the influence. And I haven't taken advantage of anyone, not even the woman who draped herself across my lap last night and asked if I could give her a ride home. I peeled her off me, called her a cab, and didn't feel a pang of regret.

I've also tried hard not to sink into self-pity, because this is the bed I made, and if I had to do it over again, I'd make it the same way. If I'd wanted it to be different, I sure as fuck could have made different decisions.

When I looked through the peephole five years ago and saw Penelope Mills standing on my doorstep, I could have not opened the door. A better man would not have opened the door.

After Maddie saw Penelope leave my apartment with her shoes and bra in her hand, I could have chased after her and begged her to forgive me for not being a better man.

But neither of those things would have *actually made me a better man.*

After the pancakes, we load Maddie's car and I follow her in the truck to Seattle, where we unload Maddie's and Gabe's few possessions into the new place. It's a solid apartment, nothing special, but sturdy and well-kept, in a good neighborhood, and just the right size for them. I tell her she did good, and she smiles, but only with the outside of her face.

Gabe dances around the apartment. He clearly loves it. He loves the window seat in the living room the most. I bet he'll come up with a million great games to play there.

Not that I'll be around much to see them. But you know.

Maddie and I stand awkwardly in the nearly empty living room. As nice as the place is, it feels blank and echoey because she doesn't have furniture. Part of me just wants to walk away, because it's not going to get any easier to say good-bye. But this other part of me can't leave them here, my people, without doing something about the emptiness and the echo. So I offer to follow her and Gabe to Ikea so they can use my truck for a shopping trip. I know Maddie was able to save a little bit by staying with me, so I figure she has enough to buy at least a few things for the apartment.

And that's weird too. The three of us out in public, doing a thing that families do, buying furniture for an apartment, but that's not how this is. It's not how it will ever be.

We go back to the apartment and haul the stuff—a couch, a table and chairs, two beds, and a night table for Maddie—into the elevator and up to the apartment. I lay the boxes out in the middle of the living room and we stand there awkwardly, until she says, "Jack. You can go."

"You're going to need some help with the assembly," I say.

"I can read Ikea instructions," she says darkly.

"It's easier with two people."

I expect her to fight, but she lets me help. And it's fun, in a hollowed-out way. All the parts laid out on the floor, passing the instructions back and forth, tossing the Allen wrench over the wreckage between us, laughing when we fuck it up.

We build Gabe's new bunk bed first, and he's like an explosion of little-boy joy, watching and "helping" us, and beside himself with excitement as we finish. I build him a fort on the lower bunk, and he takes his Legos in there, and you can hear him humming contentedly.

Next we work on Maddie's bed, and we're like a well-oiled machine now, barely speaking as we wordlessly translate the pictures on the instructions to the parts in the real world. We're in the zone, from a technical perspective.

But it still feels that same way, like something missing its soul.

I start to wish . . .

I start to wish I were this other guy. The guy who belongs here. The guy whose job it is to tighten the cams and hoist the slats into the bed frame. The guy who'll be sleeping on this bed tonight.

The better man.

And then we're done.

"You don't have to stay, Jack. We've got this. Gabe and I are going to be fine. It's a nice place, right?"

She's not quite looking at me as she says it.

"It's a great place."

My voice is too hearty.

"So—can you take him next weekend?"

"Yeah," I say. I almost say, *Do you want me to stay? Just tonight? To make sure everything's okay?* But what wouldn't be okay? It's just an apartment, and she's a competent adult. She can handle anything that happens. And I don't really want her to say no.

I don't want to hear her tell me they're fine on their own.

So I hug Gabe goodbye, and then Maddie and I stand facing each other awkwardly. I don't hug her. Because—we don't hug. Too complicated. Too much water under the bridge. You know. Like I said, originally.

And I leave.

35

MADDIE

Gabe watches as Jack goes out the front door, and then he turns to me with a question on his face, but before he can ask it, I say, "Help me cook dinner!" in one of those hyperexcited voices that adults use when they're trying to distract kids.

I don't want him to ask whatever he was about to ask, because I have no idea how to answer.

"Yeah!" he says.

I pull one of our new chairs over to the counter. "I left the step stool at Daddy's house," I tell him apologetically. "I'll get you a new one tomorrow."

"Why?"

"Why what?"

"Why you leave it at Daddy's house?"

"So you can use it when you visit Daddy there."

We've talked several times over the last few days about what was going to happen, that Gabe and I were going to move into the new apartment together and Daddy was going to stay in the house at Revere Lake. That Gabe will keep visiting Daddy on the weekends the way he always has. And Gabe has taken it more or less in stride, asking some questions but not getting upset. It's not unlike how he was about leaving Harris behind, and I thank God again that four is such a resilient age.

Dinner is one of those healthy frozen lasagna dinners and a bunch of cut-up raw veggies, which we eat at our new kitchen table. Gabe talks a mile a minute with his mouth full of chewed-up cauliflower, totally in love with his new bunk bed and the fort Jack made for him. After dinner, he tells me, he's going to play more Legos in the fort.

I'm glad he's happy and doubly glad he's so chatty. It fills the big emptiness of our new surroundings. Not that they're actually physically empty. We do still need more furniture, especially in the living area, but it's not half bad. Maybe a coffee table and a couple of floor lamps, an end table, a bookshelf—but basically, it looks like a real apartment now. No, the emptiness is more that it feels like someone's missing. I don't mean to sound like I'm being coy or in denial—I know the someone is Jack. I just also know that there's nothing I can do about it, except wait for time to take away the sense of absence.

After dinner I do the dishes, and Gabe helps again. He's actually getting pretty good at soaping and rinsing. The kitchen looks only a little bit like there's been a tsunami.

Then we do pj's and teeth, and it's surprisingly easy to convince Gabe to get in bed because of the bunk-bed fort. I crawl behind the hanging blanket and snuggle with him in the cave. It's very peaceful in there. I totally understand why he loves it.

I get him all settled—he's so sleepy that his eyes are

already doing the long-blink routine—and I'm easing myself out of the fort when he says, "Where Daddy?"

A feeling like the dentist's lead X-ray apron settles on my chest. "He's at his house. In Revere Lake."

"Why?"

No. No, please don't do this. Not now.

"Because that's where Daddy lives."

"We live there too?"

I bite my lip. Hard. I think I taste blood.

"No, baby, we live here. In this apartment. This is our new apartment."

"Why?"

"Gabe, honey, it's late, and you need to go to sleep."

"Why dis our new apartment?"

I can't. I can't comfort him about this, can't explain this to him, can't talk to him, or anyone, about this while it's so raw and fresh for me. But I have no choice, do I? He's here and I'm here and he wants to understand.

So much of parenting is about doing what needs to be done even when you don't believe you have the strength to do it, because you have to. You have to have enough strength for yourself and your kids.

"Your mommy and your daddy both love you so much. But some mommies and daddies can't live in the same house. They're not—"

I almost said, *They're not friends.* But Jack and I *are* friends.

The truth is, *Some mommies and daddies can't live in the same house because the daddy will never love the mommy as much as she wants to be loved by him.*

"We only lived in Daddy's house to give us time to find a place to stay, remember? And Mommy found a place, so now we have a place to stay, this wonderful apartment with your new bunk beds, and this is our new home. This is where we belong. And Daddy belongs in Revere Lake."

"He come here? Say g'night?"

Gabe's eyes are big, his lower lip beginning to quiver.

My chest clenches and tears fill my eyes. "No, baby. Not tonight. You'll see him in six days. That's not very long."

Gabe thinks about that hard, his little brow furrowed up. For a moment I think we're going be okay.

Then his whole serious, thoughtful face dissolves. He starts to cry. "Now. Daddy come now," he wails.

"Oh, *buddy*," I say, and all my inner walls crash down.

That's how Gabe and I end up in the fort that Jack built, curled up together, while tears stream down his face and I try to hide my own.

36

JACK

O h, *shit.*

It's Thursday morning. I've just arrived at my work site, and there's a scrum of people outside the project super's trailer. That huddle has trouble written *all* over it. The super, Kevin, is there, and the clients, and—this is the part that raises my blood pressure—Mad Max, the project developer. Max is a college-educated prick who got greedy and tried to cash in on the building boom in Revere Lake even though he doesn't know shit about construction. Part of Max's sucktastic management style is to be hands off even when a royal edict would prevent bloodshed, so the fact that he's here can't be good.

"Jack," Max calls out. "Over here."

They're all standing there with arms crossed. It's the work-site equivalent of facing a firing squad, but there's nothing I can do besides walk over and join them.

Max looks ostentatiously at his watch and then raises his eyebrows at me. *Asswipe.* I'm, like, maybe three minutes late.

"We've got a problem."

Max means, *You've* got a problem.

My eyes flick to the clients. She's a rich California transplant with a *huge* entitlement thing going on, and he's—well, let's just say I've barely heard him utter a word in his wife's presence. Which is fine, except if—when—his wife is being a total and complete asshole and he's just standing by quietly, which keeps happening.

The wife meets my eyes with a glare. The husband won't look at me. Typical. "You installed the wrong molding for the main floor ceilings," she says.

My blood is already starting to boil. In the past, I've hesitated to go toe-to-toe with her, but all that's gotten me is my pay docked to pay for mistakes that weren't mine.

"No. I installed the right molding."

She draws a hiss of breath. Not sure anyone's said *no* to her in her entire life. But I'm not going to back down this time. You know why? Because I know I'm right. I know I'm right and I have paper to back it up—notes from my conversation with Kevin and receipts from the order that I ran by Kevin right after I placed it, to double-check.

What I don't have is the original spec, signed off on by the client, because this whole project is a management clusterfuck.

Still, I've got enough to know that whatever went wrong, *it wasn't my fault.*

And the reason I have that backup? Because of Maddie. Because of what she said to me:

This is about you thinking you're not smart enough to do it. But that's bullshit. The only reason you think you aren't is because you grew up being told over and over you weren't. But it's not true.

I didn't want to hear her when she first said it, but the words stayed in my head. They echoed around every time I was at work, and they made me feel surer about certain things. They made me feel certain I was right about Max's incompetence and that Kevin's way of doing things sucked. That we needed to do things more carefully, more officially, more efficiently. Altogether fucking differently, actually.

Most of all, Maddie's words convinced me that I didn't have to take Kevin's bullshit just because I've always felt like I basically deserved whatever crap people threw in my direction.

"The only words I need to be hearing out of your mouth right now are an apology for fucking this up," Kevin growls in my direction.

Excellent. My supervisor has sold me out again.

"Seems like we all agree about that," Max says, smiling at California Girl with a submissive tilt to his head, like a whipped dog.

Any faint hope I had that Max was planning to stand up for me vanishes. So it's going to come down to my word against the clients' and Kevin's.

For a long moment, I weigh my options. I can see the writing on the wall and cave. Or I can keep going down this path that Maddie has sent me down, and see where it leads.

"Can you hang on a minute?"

The paper trail to sort this out is in my truck. I dash over to the truck, dig out the folder I've been keeping, and bring it back. I pull out the notes and the receipts. I unfold them and hand them to Max.

He looks them over, and then he looks up at me.

Then he crumples the sheets tight in his fist and says,

"Look. Jack. Leave the administrative stuff to me, hey? Your job is to hold a hammer. This is way above your pay grade."

Sometimes you just have these moments where everything aligns. Like, all of a sudden, I get this sharp visual flash of that day when we were playing Wiffle ball in the streets and my dad chewed me out about the wreaths. About the order form I'd fucked up. Another asshole, another piece of paper, another ball-busting.

But that crumpled paper in Max's hand, those pieces of paper, say I did right. I did okay.

I stand there, my arms dangling by my sides even though they all still have their body language tight and accusatory. I think about going home and telling Maddie this story, telling her what happened and what I did next.

Two things happen. My chest gets tight with grief. Because I'm not going home and telling Maddie this story. She's not at home, and she won't be, not ever again. Every day this week, I've been reminded of that fact when I walk in the door and am greeted by my silent, empty house. And no matter how much whiskey I consume at O'Hannihans, no matter how late I stay out, it's just as silent later, too.

The second thing that happens is that I realize how I want this episode with Kevin and Max and the clients to end. I understand exactly what story I would want to tell Maddie, if I could.

Calmly, I open my palm, and after a moment of hesitation, Max restores the crumpled paper to me.

"My job *was* to hold a hammer."

I say it quietly.

I say it to California Girl and Asshole Kevin and Mad Max.

I say it to my dad.

And most of all, I say it to Maddie and Gabe, who make me want to be a better person.

"I quit."

37

MADDIE

I'm meeting Sienna for drinks at a bar a couple of blocks from my new place. She had to talk me into it because I felt weird about making her come all the way into Seattle, but she said she wanted to get a peek at the apartment, and besides, it was easier for her to come into the city than for me to leave it.

When I show up at the bar, Cucumber, Lani's there, too, sitting at a table for three with Sienna.

My stomach gives a weird little skip. I don't mind hanging out with Lani, but I don't think I'd be able to stand it if she actually started talking about Jack, or if it came out that they'd hooked up again.

This has been a really tough week. As much as I tell myself I'm doing the right thing for myself and Gabe, there have been tears at every bedtime, and I don't mean Gabe's. He's actually doing okay—after that first night when he and I cried together, he seems to understand the lay of the land, though he keeps asking when he'll get to see Daddy again. It was wonderful, this morning, to finally be able to say "tomorrow night," since this is Jack's weekend, Friday and Saturday nights.

I'm dreading it, though. The hand-off. The old awkwardness, back in force. Driving away from Gabe and Jack when all I want to do is hole up with them.

Sienna stands and gives me a huge hug. "Hey, sister."

The words tug on a barely scabbed-over wound. In a different version of the world, we would have been sisters.

Lani rises, too, and hugs me. "Don't be mad."

"Why would I be mad?" I pull back to give her a quizzical look.

Sienna puts a hand on my arm. "We have something to tell you," she says, biting her lip. "I thought Lani should tell you herself."

"Um, okay?"

"Just, sit down. And we ordered you a drink. Here." Sienna pushes something pink across the table, and I pick it up and take a sip. Meanwhile, my mind is racing, trying to figure out what the heck could be going on. My instincts tell me it has to have something to do with Jack . . . like now's the moment when Lani tells me she and Jack are together.

And I'll be okay with that. I have to be, right? He never promised me anything, and I knew from the very beginning —the first very beginning—what I was getting myself into.

So why does it feel like I can barely breathe?

"Just tell me," I manage to eke out.

"You might be angry at us at first," Sienna says.

At *us*? What does Sienna have to do with it?

Lani gives me a pleading look. "It's my fault. I made her tell me."

What? What's going on?

"Sorry. We're confusing the shit out of you, aren't we?" Sienna asks.

I nod and take a big ol' drink of my pink goodness, because I'm really baffled now.

"Start at the beginning," Sienna instructs Lani.

"Okay. So, Jack's been—"

"He's been impossible," Sienna blurts. "Like, won't talk to anyone, drinking like a fish . . ."

"Grumpy as hell," Lani confirms. "And not in a needs-to-get-laid way. And I don't mean I was trying," she says, so quickly she almost trips over the words. "I wouldn't do that to you. Friends before men."

I'm honestly shocked to hear her say that. And a little, well, distrustful. Because why would this woman, who barely knows me, put loyalty to me before a guy she's known since high school? Touchily, I say, "Jack and I are over. If we ever even were."

"Oh, you were," Sienna says fervently. "You definitely were."

I'm starting to realize that whatever they want to tell me, it's not the kind of bad news I was anticipating. I take a cautiously hopeful breath.

Lani crosses her arms. "He's a fucking disaster. I've never seen him like this, Maddie. And I've known him a long time. A *long* time. I won't lie to you. That boy makes the rounds. So I feel like I speak from a place of extensive knowledge when I say that he has never tanked like this."

Sienna nods ferociously. "Cosign. He's a wreck."

"So, after a couple of days of watching him look like the grim reaper, I finally asked Sienna what the fuck was up. And she told me she was pretty sure it had something to do with you. Which, I will honestly say, I was not surprised to hear. I thought there was something pretty fishy about how he's been ever since you moved in—"

"I didn't move in." My voice has, once again, come out testier than I intended. "I—I was just crashing."

"Whatever." Lani waves her hand. "He's been different since you moved in, and I was starting to get the feeling something was going on, and so when Sienna told me the two of you were sleeping together, I was actually relieved—like, okay, he's not dying of cancer, or whatever. But then when she told me that you'd moved out, I was all, like, *what the fuck?*"

"So I told her what you told me," Sienna says apologetically. "I'm sorry. I usually am good with other people's secrets, but before you decide you don't want to be my friend anymore—"

"—or mine—" Lani adds.

"—just hear Lani out."

"So she told me your story, and right away, I was like, oh, I bet that woman, with the shoes and the bra, that was Penelope Mills. She had the hots for Jack that summer. She spent, like, the whole summer trying to get into his pants, and she was *bullshit* when she found out that he was with you—"

"Not *with* me," I amend. *Penelope Mills.* Now the blonde with the shoes and the bra has a name, and it doesn't make me feel any better.

"*With* you," Sienna insists.

"So, here's the part where you get up and walk out," Lani says.

"I'm not going to get up and walk out."

"No, because it's not your style. You're too nice. But you

might want to after I tell you the rest." Lani takes a big breath. "I messaged her. On FB."

"You—?"

"I messaged Penelope Mills. We were never really good friends, but we are Facebook friends, and I figured given the situation it wouldn't be too weird to ask her if she'd ever slept with Jack—"

"You *what*?" I screech.

"I asked her if she'd ever slept with Jack."

Lani looks like she wishes the floor would swallow her. And I'm mad enough that she's probably right to wish it.

"I can't believe you!"

But I'm gradually starting to calm down as I realize that they didn't get me here and feed me a pink drink so they could tell me what I already know.

Or believed I knew.

And for the first time, it registers, what they were saying earlier. Jack is a mess. Drinking, sulking, *not hooking up.*

Jack misses me.

I feel a flutter of stupid but very real hope.

"He was a mess after you left the first time," Sienna says quietly. "He always said you caught him with someone else and that's why it didn't work out between you, but it never added up for me. I just felt like there was more to the story. So when Lani said she knew Penelope and she could ask her, I told her to do it."

"What—what did she say?"

My voice is so small, I almost don't recognize it.

Lani lays her palm on the table in front of me. "Penelope went to Jack's apartment to seduce him. I guess she started taking her clothes off, but he said he wasn't interested. He said he was with you. He made her get dressed and he threw her out."

"That's what you saw," Sienna tells me triumphantly. "Penelope striking out."

Once again, I'm having a lot of trouble catching my breath.

"But—"

I try again. "But—I—he—why didn't he just tell me that?"

They're both shaking their heads.

"You're sure. You're sure Penelope wouldn't lie about that?"

Lani makes a scoffing noise. "There is no way Penelope slept with Jack. Penelope and I were very competitive in high school about our conquests, and if she had a chance to tell me she'd slept with Jack, she would have jumped at the opportunity."

My world is rearranging itself around me, and not in an entirely pleasing way. "He *let me think*—he was okay with me believing—"

"I think you and Jack have some things to talk about," Sienna murmurs.

I tip the rest of my drink back and set the empty glass on the table with a solid thunk.

"*That's* an understatement."

38

JACK

"Can't," I say.

Henry squints. "You can't go out."

He, Chase, and Brooks are standing on my front stoop. Henry's truck is idling in the driveway. They obviously thought this would be more of an in-and-out mission than it's turning out to be.

"Gotta save. It's all sandwiches and cheap beer until the business starts bringing in money."

I have spent the last couple of days making phone calls, the first baby steps toward becoming a general contractor and business owner. It's pretty exhilarating. It's not going to be easy. I'm going to be eating a lot of peanut butter and tuna fish and forgoing nights out for a long time, but my finances and credit are good, my work history is solid, and I played high school football with the business loan officer at the local bank. Never hurts.

Henry wanted to quit Kevin's crew too, in solidarity, but I told him to wait. I told them I'd hire him as soon as I could, but in the meantime, he should keep making steady money.

Henry gives me the stink eye. "So basically, you just became a free man again, and now you can't have fun because you're cheap."

I flip him the finger.

"So, seriously, you're not going to O'Hannihans with us?"

"Seriously," I say.

He rolls his eyes and sighs. "Fine, then. It's gonna have to be pizza and cheap beers here."

I think he's afraid if he leaves me alone here, I'll fall apart, what with how I've been since Maddie left and the whole temporarily unemployed bit. But I'm actually feeling pretty optimistic for the first time in a while. It's good to have a plan.

Henry goes back outside to kill the truck engine and the four of us end up sitting around my living room, putting back Bud Lights, watching basketball, and destroying a large pizza.

The last of the pizza has just slid down Henry's gullet when there's a knock at the front door.

"You expecting anyone?" Brooks asks, looking hopeful. Like I've arranged for a troupe of strippers without mentioning it, possibly.

I shake my head.

I get to my feet and head to the door, figuring worst case, my mother or my sister dropping in; best case, Lani taking my temperature to see if I'm back to being a willing fuck buddy (No. That train left the station.).

Only, you know.

It's Maddie.

Suddenly there's this crazy jumble in my chest, this mixed-up salad of everything I've ever felt for her or about her. What she meant to me when we were kids and how bad I've wanted her as long as I've known how to want anyone and how good it felt to be with her and how bad it feels not to be. And I want to, I don't know, get down on my knees and beg, but also slam the door in her face.

She looks so good. She's wearing work clothes, some green blouse-thing shot through with silver over a slim, short black skirt and heels.

Her face is flushed, her eyes bright—

"Did you sleep with her?"

She's pissed.

"What?" I'm wracking my brains for anyone she could legitimately be talking about, but the last person I slept with was so utterly and thoroughly her that my mind is basically a blank.

"Penelope Mills. Did you sleep with her?"

For a moment the name doesn't even register, and then I remember. Penelope Mills.

I think she sees the truth on my face right then, but she keeps at it. "Did you? Jack. Answer me. *Did you sleep with her?"*

She's so intense. Like it was twenty seconds ago and not five years ago that Penelope Mills walked out of my apartment with her shoes and her bra in her hand. Like it still matters that much. And the thing is, it does, and I know it too.

From behind me I hear whispering and rustling, and then Henry and Brooks materialize and slink around us, toward the door. "Time for us to be going," Henry says, wincing in my direction. *Sorry, man,* he mouths.

But I'm not sorry. Not really. I can't be sorry to see her. I've wanted this every moment of every day since I walked out of her and Gabe's new place, without realizing how much. And even if she's angry, she's here.

As soon as the guys are gone, she resumes the inquisition.

"Did. You. Sleep. With. Her?"

I should have told her the truth. So many times. And it's probably too late now—I think the rules are that if she comes to your house and shouts in your face, it's too late, but regardless, it's our moment of truth. This week, I stood up for myself and began to remake my life, for better or for worse, because of her, because of the kind of woman she is and the kind of man I want to be for her and our son, and I can't lie to her again, not even by omission. I will never, ever lie to her again, not even by omission.

I shake my head. "No."

Her eyes get bigger. "Did you even kiss her?"

"No."

"Did anything happen between you?"

"She—she took her dress off. And—her bra."

It's funny—even though she's creeping close to the truth, I feel as guilty as I ever have. Guiltier. Because of the look on her face. Like we're finally getting down to the real nature of my betrayal.

"And then I made her put her dress back on. And I threw her out."

It feels good to say it. Right. Freeing. I wonder if it always would have felt like this, or if it had to come down to this moment.

She shakes her head angrily. "Jack, why? Why—why would you do that? Why would you let me think you had if you hadn't?"

I don't know how to answer. It's like the words are trapped behind a barricade.

"Jesus, Jack, how could you? How could you *do* that?"

Suddenly, she's crying. And coming toward me. Pounding her fists against my chest, raining blows on me, sobbing. "You broke my heart!"

There's really only one thing to do, as there is only ever one thing that I can do when Maddie cries. I gather her in my arms, trying to contain the flailing fists and the hiccupy sobs and all the rage coming off her in waves.

"You let me think—" *Sob.*

"I was *pregnant!*" *Gasp.*

"I can't believe you!"

And then more sobs, her body shuddering in my arms.

Gradually, she calms down.

"Why?" She pulls away. "Why would you do that? Did you do it to get rid of me? To get rid of me and Gabe? You didn't have to do that. You could have just said you didn't want to be involved."

I'm shaking my head. "No. No!"

"Then why?"

I understand now why I've avoided this conversation for so long. Because the answer to her question is such a small, mean thing. I'm ashamed of how tiny and twisted my heart is.

"When you looked at me like that—"

If this is what it feels like to be a real man, it fucking sucks. My voice breaks on the words, and I want to pull the shutters closed between us so she doesn't see if the rest of me breaks, too.

"Like what?"

Her voice is much gentler now, like she knows. Like she

knows how close to the edge I am. And maybe, maybe—like she knows that she's the only person who can get me here, the only person I will ever let see me like this.

"You trusted me."

She shakes her head, confused.

"You always trusted me. And then, at the lake, at the boathouse, you trusted me with *you*. With your feelings, with your body. But when you saw Penelope leaving my apartment, you looked at me the way everyone always looked at me, like I was a mistake."

A little breath whooshes out of her. Her eyes are huge. I should stop—I'm hurting her—but I can't.

"You were the only one who'd ever had that kind of faith in me. And I knew. Even if it wasn't Penelope, it was going to be someone. Or something. I'd hurt you, I'd hurt the baby, I'd screw us up. It was just a matter of time, and then what you were thinking about me that night would be true. And I just —" My voice breaks again, but I have to finish. I have to explain, as little sense as it will probably make to her.

"I couldn't."

39

MADDIE

e's turned away from me now, like he can't bear to look at me. Like I might have that look on my face again. And I think about Jack, the Jack I've known since he was still a boy, as full of promise and joy as Gabe is now, and how his father slowly sapped his faith in himself. How Jack's father wore him down, like a river over stone, eroding his ability to see the best in himself.

For a long time I believed it was my job to keep that faith, that ability, alive for Jack.

But in the end, when it mattered . . .

So now I understand. I understand what happened that night. And I feel so much relief, and also so much guilt and grief.

"I didn't trust you. I didn't believe in you. When you needed me to."

He very slowly looks up at me, and the expression on his face—it's simultaneously so broken and so hopeful.

I take a deep breath. Because there are a lot of layers here.

There's a lot of talking that needs to be done, a lot of sorting-out that needs to happen.

"I owed you the benefit of the doubt," I say, slowly. "Not just a chance to explain yourself, but the benefit of the doubt. Because of how it was between us. And Jack, it was *so* good between us. So good."

He's quiet, still, just listening to me.

"But—I was scared, Jack. I didn't know you very well. I mean, for all that I'd known you forever, I didn't know the adult you. All I knew about you were the rumors, and they—"

"They weren't flattering."

"They weren't. And I wanted to believe I was different from all the other disposable women, but—then I had this evidence right in front of my face that I wasn't different. And I —I wasn't bigger than my fear, I guess."

He looks an awful lot like Gabe does when you're answering his *why* questions. Just eyes and attention, his face so vulnerable and downright—sweet.

"Neither was I." He takes a deep breath. "You *are* different from all the other disposable women. You are different from every other woman. It was only ever you. And it will only ever be you. And the only thing I regret more than letting you walk away that night is letting you move out of my house last weekend."

My heart is suddenly three sizes too big. "Oh."

"And I just want you to know that I'll do whatever it takes. Work on my temper—"

"Your . . . temper?"

I'm genuinely befuddled.

"The other night, when Gabe wouldn't go to bed, and I lost it?"

"Was I there?"

"You were standing right there. And I was like, trembling with rage—"

"Oh, yeah, those bedtime shenanigans can make you lose your shit."

"In my head, I could see my dad, shouting at me, getting in my face—"

His voice cracks. His eyes are agonized. And it takes me a moment, but then I get it. I get that for him, that moment felt so real and so familiar, it broke his heart.

I reach for his hand, grab it tight. "You know it doesn't count if you don't actually *do* it, right? I mean, if it did, he would be dead from shaken baby syndrome a thousand times over. I can't tell you the number of times I had to walk out of the room when he was a baby because I was scared I'd do something awful to him."

"But how did you know you wouldn't? One day? Some day?"

"I just—I knew, you know?"

"No," he says. "I don't."

And I look at him, like I'm seeing him for the first time, and I think I *am* seeing him for the first time. Hair just long enough to wave, eyes the blue-gray of a cloudy day's ocean, features set in steel, including a jaw clenched so tight I'm afraid something's going to crack.

"Oh, Jack," I say, reaching out to touch the evening's early stubble along his rigid jawline. "*I* know."

He drags in a deep breath.

"I know you will never hurt us. And if I could go back, and never have had my faith in you flag, not even for a millisecond, not in any way, I would."

He closes his eyes, just for a second, then opens them again. It might just be my imagination, but they look damp. Which makes my own heart feel like it's going to burst.

"Just because I did that one stupid, idiotic thing and let myself believe that you would sleep with stupid Penelope Mills does not mean that I ever thought you wouldn't be a good father. You are *not* your father. You couldn't be your father if you tried. You are the very best father."

Now it's my turn to draw a shaky breath. "You are the man I want to teach Gabe how to be a man."

He leans his face into my hand. Turns his head just a little, so he can press his lips against my palm. They're warm and gentle, and that touch sizzles straight through me.

When he lifts his head again, his eyes are warm, and I can see the tension has melted out of his jaw.

He smiles wryly at me.

"Even though I'm unemployed?"

40

JACK

I tell her about the confrontation.

"Those *bastards*," she breathes.

I tell her about the paper trail and the way Max crumpled it.

"That *asshole!*"

And then I tell her what happened next. It's not easy to say. I guess I'm finally learning that it's pretty hard for me to tell Maddie, or anyone, how I feel.

"You know how you said I should start my own business?"

She nods.

"I've been thinking about it. I've been doing some research and taking some steps. So when Max crumpled up those pieces of paper, I just—knew. I was going to do it."

And here's the hard part.

"I knew, because I wanted to be that guy. That guy you were describing. The one who was smart, who wouldn't take shit from the super or the developer."

Nope. Here's the hard part.

"I wanted to be that guy *for you.*"

"Oh," she says again, but this time her eyes shine with tears.

Okay, I think I've earned this. I slide my hand into the back of her hair and draw her close and kiss her hard. And oh, my God, it's good. Her mouth is sweet and hungry, and how did just a few days without doing this become unbearable?

Then, just as I'm about to pick her up and deposit her on a soft horizontal surface and have my wicked way with her, she pulls back and gives me a suspicious look.

"But you dismissed the idea of starting your own business when I said it."

"Yes. I dismissed the idea at the time."

She grins. "So . . .?"

"Okay. You told me so."

"I told you so!"

"Just don't make that a habit," I say gruffly, but I don't fucking care. She can lord everything over me for the rest of our lives, and that will be okay. Because, let's just repeat that. *Rest of our lives!*

And I realize—I'm here, telling her the story, just the way I wanted to when it happened. I'm home, she's home, we're home together, and—

"Where's Gabe?"

"Sienna's there."

"How?"

"Don't ask," she says. "Your sister is a good person. I love her. Keep talking."

She loves Sienna, huh?

Does she love *me*?

Maybe she's feeling it too, because she says, "So, Jack. Just to clarify. We're, like, together."

"We're actually fucking together," I clarify. "Not just 'like.'"

"Like, we're going to live together in the same house with Gabe?"

"That. Exactly fucking that. No 'like' about it."

"And we're going to have sex." Her voice drops, and she gets this super-sexy secret smile on her face.

"Lots of sex," I say.

"Could we, um, start now?"

I don't bother to answer that question. Or, not in words, anyway. I cup her face in my hands and drop my mouth to hers, and kiss her as gently as I can manage. Which lasts about three seconds, because she grabs the back of my head and pulls on my hair and kisses me *so* fucking fiercely that I have trouble catching my breath.

No one kisses like Maddie. Like she's all in, like all of her energy and spirit is focused into making me feel as good as humanly possible, like she's trying to tell me with her lips and her tongue how much I matter to her. And I'm trying to tell her back. We're tangled up, getting in each other's way; it's like a wrestling match as we tumble onto the couch, and she's trying to get my clothes off and I'm trying to get hers off, and I think we end up tying the whole batch into a knot. Then somehow we're actually naked, or at least naked enough, and I've got my face buried in her breasts, in the satin feel of her. I drink in her scent, loving the contrasts, her smooth cool skin and hot tight nipples under my tongue, and—

"Fuck me, fuck me, fuck me," she murmurs.

"Excuse me?"

"You heard me."

She tips her hips up and rubs herself against me, reaching down to arrange us so I can slide through her wetness without actually penetrating, but that makes us both gasp. She squirms under me until it feels like my two choices are embarrass myself or just do it, so when her hips tilt so the head of my dick lines up perfectly with her sex, I thrust.

She starts coming, arching and panting and spasming around me, and—

"Oh, *shit,* Maddie, don't do that—"

Because I'm losing it now, the orgasm surging up, and even though it feels so damn good, losing myself in her, pouring myself into her, I think I wanted it to last forever, this feeling that she is finally, finally, mine.

As I come down, teetering in that weird almost-disappointment, she whispers something against my ear.

"What?"

"I said, 'I love you, Jack Parker.'"

Oh. Okay, then. Scratch the whole disappointed thing.

I brace myself on one arm and brush her hair back from her face, smiling down at her. "I love you, too."

It doesn't feel scary. It feels like I've told her a hundred times before in a hundred different ways, and if I haven't?

I fucking should have, because it's always been true.

EPILOGUE

ONE YEAR LATER — JACK

It's bring-Gabe-to-work day. This is an unofficial holiday I've declared because every night when I get home from work, he demands to know when he can come see the houses I'm working on. It's been a little tricky because, well, I don't want him to see the houses before Maddie does.

But today she's home from work for her twenty-week ultrasound, which is where the three of us will go as soon as we're done here, and—

Oh, I'm sorry, did I leave that part out?

Right. So. Maddie is pregnant.

We decided we couldn't let Gabe get too complacent with his only-child status. Plus Sienna and my mom kept asking for more babies and we didn't want to disappoint. Just kidding. About the not-wanting-to-disappoint part. The harassment was real. And relentless.

Maddie and Gabe get out of her car and come up to the trailer-office.

"Daddy!" Gabe yells, catapulting himself into my arms.

"Hey, Jack," Maddie says, strolling up behind him, giving me a private smile that goes straight to my dick.

Maddie is just starting to look pregnant, and I get a sick, alpha-male kick out of having knocked her up. Also because her tits are epic. I may have to keep her pregnant for the rest of her fertile life. She actually might not mind. It's been a good pregnancy and she loves feeling the baby kick (as does Gabe), and she is so horny that she is asking for sex twice a day (and once confessed to making herself come pretty much every time she's alone, which is such a fucking turn-on that I keep coming up with excuses to take Gabe to the playground and the five-and-ten, and . . . yeah).

Other things that have happened since last we met: I got my general contractor's license. Studying for that exam was the hardest thing I've ever done except for telling Maddie the truth about not cheating on her (which is still a thing that makes me raise one eyebrow at myself in disbelief). Luckily, Maddie's faith in me never once wavered, even when the two of us were up night after night with her quizzing me. Gabe even got in on the action and would pop-quiz me on stuff Maddie had primed him on.

I almost threw up in the testing room, but I passed.

Also, Harris dumped Mia. I'm sure you could have seen that one coming, because once an asshole, always an asshole. Mia and Harris lasted about two months after Maddie caught them dining in. Then Harris said that he'd never been *that* into her, really, that his therapist thought maybe he'd just been using Mia to get out of his commitment to Maddie.

Ouch. Like, *ouch, ouch,* ouch.

Mia asked Maddie if she'd be willing to give her another

chance. She said she didn't expect forgiveness or even trust, but she'd really, really like to meet for a cup of coffee. So they've been doing that. Coffee. Maddie says it'll be a long time before she trusts Mia with anything that matters, and I think it's good to be cautious, but I also think they'll be okay, someday. And I'm in favor of it, Maddie forgiving Mia. Everyone makes mistakes, and love can make us really, really stupid.

It can also make us our best selves. I should know.

"Hey," I say, as they reach the trailer. I let Gabe come inside and look around (although there's nothing exciting about it—just desks and computers and blueprints and files, the most complete records of everything that happens anywhere on my building site that you can imagine). He sits in my chair and spins it around, and then he asks to see inside the houses.

Most of the other houses being built in Revere Lake right now are McMansions, but I chose to work with this developer on my first big project because he wanted to build not-so-big and more affordable designs. And we're both pretty damn excited about the houses that are coming out of our collaboration. They've got relatively small footprints but a great open feel, lots of light, lots of nooks and crannies for kids and storage. They're all built with high-quality materials, often repurposed—and they all sold within a couple of days of us finishing the model house.

Luckily, I can still tell Gabe he can see inside the houses, because there is one house that, even though it's sold, isn't yet occupied. The new owners are waiting to move in because—well, because.

So we head down to the end of the cul-de-sac.

This one is my favorite. It backs up on wooded conservation land, which means that no matter how developed Revere Lake gets, this house will keep its secluded, private feel and its beautiful view overlooking a little stream. It has the best light of any house in the development, because I personally made sure the angle of the house on the lot brought in plenty of sun and no direct views of its neighbors.

I open the front door and lead them inside. The main floor has an open design and the second floor overlooks it from a balcony, so the foyer feels big and open and flooded with light even though it's not actually that big in terms of square footage. Gabe squeals over the balcony and runs up the stairs right away so he can look out from between the railings. I made sure the railings were spaced so there was no way he could poke his head through.

I lead Maddie into the kitchen, which is small but efficient. Good appliances, solid cabinetry, excellent countertop materials—but not the ones that are trendy and expensive. Ones that are worth their cost.

"This is *nice*," she says wistfully. She runs a hand over the glossy surface of the countertop and touches the controls on the stove.

"Could you picture yourself making dinner here?" I ask.

She laughs. "I wish."

"Do you?"

"I'd love to live here. It's beautiful."

I smile and watch her as she explores the space—the kitchen opens into the dining and living areas, and there's a little bathroom and a small TV/away room tucked into the corner. She goes up the stairs, and I follow, admiring the rear view, watching as she and Gabe tuck their curious faces into the spaces. There are built-in bunks in one of the kids' bedrooms and the other is painted to be a nursery. There's a third kids' bedroom, too. Thinking ahead, you know?

And then she turns into the master bedroom and comes to a dead stop in the doorway. Gabe crashes into her from behind and wraps his arms around her leg to restore his balance.

There's a bed in there, and it's made up. I made it up to exactly match the bedroom in our house (the Revere Lake house formerly known as "my house"). And just in case she didn't get the point, I folded a pair of my pj's on the left-side pillow and a pair of her pj's—

Although, I'm not sure you could actually call them pj's. Remember that bodysuit, consisting mainly of black leather straps, and not so terribly many of them, that she liberated from Harris's house?

I have become much better acquainted with it of late. Anyway, it's on the right-hand pillow. (Not that she doesn't already know how much I appreciate it. I have made that abundantly clear.)

"Jack?"

Her gaze bounces from my face to the bed and back. She's clearly trying to figure out if it means what she thinks it means, and for a moment I panic. What if it's not what she wants? A house is a pretty big gift not to consult her on.

But then she throws her arms around my neck and kisses me in a way that I'm pretty sure indicates a yes.

She pulls back. "For real, Jack? This is ours?"

I nod. It's occurred to me that I'm choked up enough that if I try to actually answer, I'll sound like a tool.

"Oh, my *God,* Jack, I love it. I *love* it."

Her eyes fill suddenly with tears.

"Oh," I say. "Oh, no. Don't cry. You can't cry. Think of the children."

BONUS EPILOGUE
JACK—MANY MONTHS EARLIER

"No," Brooks says. "Whatever your excuse is, it's not good enough."

For once, I'm not the one in the hot seat. This time, it's Chase's turn.

We're doing our now-ritual bagged lunch get-together, eating this time on a cluster of large rocks near the development I just broke ground on. A development that I have some very special plans for. Right now, though, it's mostly just dirt —and these very convenient picnic rocks.

Brooks, with his special gift for making sports opportunities appear from nowhere, is holding his phone aloft to show us four Mariners tickets for tonight's game, which he won by calling into a radio show.

And Chase is shaking his head.

"Can't," he says.

"What do you mean 'can't'?" Brooks demands.

"No babysitter?" I ask him sympathetically. I pull my phone out, set it on my thigh, and surreptitiously fire off two texts. Finding good child care is a problem I've recently become an expert at solving.

A strange look comes over Chase's face. "Not exactly," he says.

Henry scowls. "Explain."

"I had to let our nanny go."

All our eyebrows go up. I have to admit, as a dad—albeit no longer a single one—I feel his pain to the depths of my soul. I remind myself to give our regular sitter a raise and send her some dark chocolate and wine.

"What happened?" I ask—because employee retention is very important and I need to know exactly how Chase screwed up so I can never, ever do it.

Chase shakes his head. "She needs some time to sort some things out."

I can tell that's all he's going to say, so I drop it, just as my phone buzzes twice in rapid succession.

"Our babysitter is free," I say, holding up my own phone triumphantly. Both texts bore fruit. Maddie has said she's happy to be on duty tonight so I can go to the game, and our regular sitter said she'd love to help Chase out.

Chase winces. "Um, yeah. Well. Here's the thing. I actually *have* a substitute nanny. A temporary one. Liv is nannying for Katie for a couple of weeks."

"Wait," Brooks says. "Liv? Like your friend Liv? The one with the red hair? The hot-as-fire one? The one who you claim is 'just a friend' but won't let me hit on?"

"I won't let you hit on her because she's my friend and you're a dog," Chase growls.

Brooks shuts one eye and gives him a doubtful look. And I have to say, I think I might side with Brooks on this one. Brooks may be a dog—or at least not the first guy you'd fix your best female friend or sister up with—but Chase gets way too fired up whenever Brooks teases him that he's going to ask Liv out. Especially because it's a hundred percent clear Brooks is deliberately riling Chase up.

Not that it's not entertaining. It is. I'd enter to win tickets to that.

"Okay, so what's the problem? Liv can watch Katie, right?" Henry asks.

Chase gets a really pained look on his face. "I, um, promised them I'd be home tonight."

Brooks's mouth drops open. "You what?"

"Liv said she and Katie made me dinner, so I promised I'd be home."

Brooks's squint gets even deeper. "Home for dinner."

"It's not like that," Chase insists. "It's just a thing she's doing with Katie, or something."

"Suuuuure it is," Henry says.

"It is!" Chase insists. "Liv and I are just friends. Neither of us is interested in making it anything other than that."

"I feel like I said something very similar to that not that long ago," I mutter, but no one is listening to me because they are all totally fixated on Chase. Understandably.

Chase crosses his arms. "Besides, she's leaving. She's going to Colorado. But her car broke down and she needs money, and I needed a nanny, so she's temporarily filling in. Just for two weeks. That's all this is. A deal to get us both through a bad time."

"Convenient," Brooks says.

"Not convenient for us," Henry says. "Very inconvenient

for us. Are you sure this dinner thing needs you? Are you sure you can't bail?"

"I'm sure," Chase says.

He doesn't hesitate. He doesn't look like he's thinking about it, weighing the pleasures of a Mariners game on a gorgeous sunny night against whatever Katie and Liv have planned for him.

And that's when I know.

Whether he knows it or not—and I'm pretty sure he still doesn't know it—Chase is not going to be a bona fide member of the single dad's survival club for much longer.

ACKNOWLEDGMENTS

Do Over, *Head Over Heels*, and *Sleepover* were first published in 2018. But re-releasing a book is its own special kind of project, and I have many people to thank for their help in making this edition possible!

First of all, many thanks to my readers for always being along for the ride! I do this for you, and I'm so grateful every time I get an email, message, or smoke signal from the ether telling me these characters have meant as much to you as they have to me.

Mr. Bell and our kids usually get the last place in my acknowledgments, which isn't fair at all, because they have first place in my heart. They're unfailingly patient and supportive and in every way the best family an author—or anyone—could want. I love you all so much.

Thank you so much to Dylann Crush, Kate Davies, and Claire Marti for being my awesome readers this time around! Thank you for taking time away from your own words to help make this book the best it could be.

Huge thanks also to the author friends who support me on a regular basis—Dylann, Megan Ryder, Christina Hovland,

Brenda St. John Brown, Claire, Christine D'Abo, Gwen Hernandez, Rachel Grant, Kate, Kris Kennedy, Karen Booth, Susannah Nix, Stina Lindenblatt, and many, many more, including but not limited to the authors of the Girls' Night In Book Club, the Corner of Smart and Sexy, Small Town World Domination, Wide for the Win, Awesome Babes for Good Things, and the RAM Rom-Com group.

Thank you to my agent, Emily Sylvan Kim, and my sub rights agent, Tina Shen, who work to make things happen for me behind the scenes!

I cannot imagine doing any of my jobs without the love and support of my parents and my amazing friends, Aimee, Chelsea, Cheryl, Darya, Ellen, Gail, Jess, Julia, Kathy, Lauren, Molly, Soomie, and Tracey. Love you!

Still So Hot!

Hot & Bothered

Standalone

Turn Up the Heat

ABOUT THE AUTHOR

USA Today bestselling author Serena Bell writes contemporary romance with heat, heart, and humor. A former journalist, Serena has always believed that everyone has an amazing story to tell if you listen carefully, and you can often find her scribbling in her tiny garret office, mainlining chocolate and bringing to life the tales in her head.

Serena's books have earned many honors, including a RITA finalist spot, an RT Reviewers' Choice Award, Apple Books Best Book of the Month, and Amazon Best Book of the Year for Romance.

When not writing, Serena loves to spend time with her college-sweetheart husband and two hilarious kiddos—all of whom are incredibly tolerant not just of Serena's imaginary friends but also of how often she changes her hobbies and how passionately she embraces the new ones. These days, it's stand-up paddle boarding, board-gaming, meditation, and long walks with good friends.